THE HUMAN
MOSAIC
OF BALMAIN

Roger Juchau

To all my grandchildren – Luca, Lia, Rylan, Louis, Marco,
Evie and Emile

Acknowledgement

I have long harboured a desire to do some fiction writing. For most of my adult life I have been involved in professional writing, rarely departing into the world of subjectivity. Ever since reading the great novels of John Updike I have sometimes mused about the lives and characters of those I have observed and encountered. I now have put this in writing. Many have heard my speculations about the region's characters I have seen and I thank them for their forbearance. Trish, Barry, Kay, Mac, Ron, Peter, Murray, Jack, Dianne, Warwick, Ross, Clyde, Deb, Susan, Andrew, Karl have all wondered who are the people I have fictionally described. My family have also had a taste of my fictional human parade. My cartoonist Peter Byrne has done a great job in providing a cartoonist interpretation of some of the characters I described. I thank him. As usual my publisher, Evan Shapiro, has been of great help. I thank my wife, Madeleine, for review and edit work for which I am eternally grateful. Finally, I want to register the privilege I have had over the last 30 years enjoying Balmain and its adjacent localities of Birchgrove and Rozelle. A community that continues to offer a welcoming life to all who decide to reside, work or linger there.

Preamble

I have been fascinated by the people of Sydney's Inner West, particularly the Balmain region. For 30 years I have lived in this region enjoying lengthy walks and coffee breaks while watching my fellow citizens navigate their lives and undertake various tasks around their suburb.

I have tried to enter their world by imagining who they are, their personalities, relationships, values and backgrounds. I have never met them. Through fictional urgings I've given them fictional names and features letting my imagination run wild to sketch them in writing. I've also given some descriptions to my cartoonist to draw them as imagined from my description.

Observing humans is a long -practised art. History has yielded hosts of writers who have observed the people around them and conjectured about their lives and character. Noticing strangers from a distance and constructing their living profiles force writers to come to an understanding of their own humanity and their own rationales for life.

The human parade is a rich source of ideas about the human condition and how social interactions shape personal journeys. The prospects of life are in a sense both limiting and limitless. As I observed my local inhabitants, I continually felt that some had a clear agenda for life while others had not yet fully realised or formed one. I felt some were conducting their lives in a reactionary and somewhat non-strategic way and I had a sense some could be socially trapped or captured, facing real barriers to break away and experience a different life.

Watching my characters forced me to think about how they enjoyed life and what brought positive feelings about themselves. I had to keep checking myself and querying why occasionally I saw negative aspects of their lives. Maybe I was influenced by my own experiences and the sub conscious intrusions of the media, carrying negative personal stories about urban life in Sydney.

Accessing their lives directly through regular personal interactions, conversing, diaries or social media entries would of course create a picture different from the ones I have fictionally composed. But perhaps my speculation from afar could have correspondence with lives led.

Concentrated and crowded urban living is a potent factor in shaping perceptions of those casually encountered or observed. You can note physical features, recurring attire, regular habits, overt mannerisms, and sometimes even their moods and feelings when conversations are accidentally overheard. Some writers believe you can make reasonable guesstimates of the state of moods by looking at a person's gait, deportment, attire, facial expressions and physical gestures. In recent times there has been research on inferring the mood and feelings of strangers through systematic scrutiny of their faces.

The persons described drew my attention because they stood out from others regularly encountered. There was something distinctive about them. They had a bearing which suggested that they had a personal history open to fictional exposition. They alerted my curiosity because in a theatrical sense they had come onto my urban stage and their roles and character demanded an illuminating script. They were part of and apart from Sydney's Inner West throng.

My Balmain Domain

The characters of my domain are found around Balmain and the adjacent localities of Birchgrove and Rozelle. Architecturally their buildings span three centuries, encompassing residential, industrial, civic and commercial sites. Industry has shrunk, yielding to housing and commerce. The ghosts of their colonial past and traces of once thriving industries of mining, power stations, refining and shipyards remain. Buildings of special heritage value are preserved, often housing business or cultural enterprises. Architecture has reflected the peninsularity of their harbourside location with its coves, bays, points and inlets. The preponderance of historic, narrow residential streets has no sympathy for large vehicles and parking space is at a premium given the absence of garages.

Nineteenth century premises have either been removed or undergone transformation in use, fabric and scale. Vestiges of the colonial housing of the middle and working classes remain in the form of cottages, terraces, lodgings and ridge-line houses and villas. Commercial vestiges are represented by strip and corner shops. Pubs, a renowned feature of the area, are in decline and closures have occurred. Remnant industry is seen in workshops and marine service facilities. Surviving community assets include churches, halls, schools, and buildings devoted to civic services such as a post office, library, police and banks. Some open spaces and foreshore areas retain elements of early settlement including heritage buildings for welfare services and water sports.

Transformation and growth in the locality had its impetus through largely demographic pulses. Changes in transport and work arrangements together with growing affluence and cultural aspirations have brought new waves of residents into the locality in the last forty years. High property prices reflect the push to relocate to the Inner West.

The housing stock has increased through high-rise apartments and town-houses. Old-time residences are becoming less evident and some public housing remains. The residential mix cuts across age, class, wealth, family, employment and gender categories. Historically it is largely of European heritage. Amongst the empty nesters, single households and families, a more diverse and multicultural community is becoming visible. Some observers see the locality as a bit of a haven for professionals and artists, many of whom align with social reform politics. Pockets of activists pursue welfare, justice and freedom causes. Traditionally a strong Labor Party community it is now more politically diverse embracing views across the liberal and conservative spectrum.

Shopping precincts are in transition revealing vacant shops, mushrooming food and coffee shops, salons, pop-up shops and other services shops with a tenuous grip. The bountiful number of medical and health practitioners are supported by the presence of a small public hospital and rehabilitation centre. The once vibrant pub scene is a shadow of its former self. On weekends the human parade undergoes a change along the high street where the young and middle aged outnumber the elderly. Many share a love of canines when, on occasions, it is impossible to discern whether it is the owner or pet controlling the leash.

The region's denizens are a rich tapestry of urban dwellers. Amongst this urban throng can be found flag carriers for various causes, relationship arrangements of all hues, active senior groups, many stay-at-home Dads, exercise zealots, dabblers in the arts, cuisine experimenters, phalanxes of coffee bearers, prolific renovators, park enthusiasts, passionate perambulators, tenants in flux and residents remembering the good old days. They appear comfortable in its compact surrounds and recognise the value of its indigenous and colonial heritage. They enjoy also an enviable supply of reliable public transport links to the metropolis.

THE CHARACTERS

Sam

Sam can be found sitting alone most Saturday mornings at his local pub, enjoying his regular schooner of beer whilst scanning the racing form and occasionally glancing up to view the other morning drinkers, whose numbers have increasingly dwindled over time. Absent now are the old regulars soaking up their morning schooners and enjoying their fags. He misses the old-time barmaids who would enquire about his health as well as the venting of their views about the state of politics. Enjoyed was their earthy and wry humour and particularly their commentary on the sexual inadequacies of those younger male patrons who boast of their deeds with the opposite sex. The current batch of younger barmaids seem to him remote and devoid of character.

Sam is roughly shaved and, irrespective of the outside temperature, wears his grey cardigan to counter draughts and air conditioning. The pub is his main social outlet since he became a widower 11 years ago. Now 73 years old, he often reflects on his working life with Sydney ferries and the lack of contact with his unmarried daughter. His nick name at work was Sambo. Was it because of his crinkly hair and dark complexion or was it because of his name? He never found out. He had few friends at work. He blamed his height and weight for not succeeding in sport, especially rugby league, his favourite sport. At five foot seven, nine and half stone, shy and inarticulate, Sam was never the person who attracted companionship.

His late wife never gave Sam real companionship. She had sisters and nieces with whom she would spend time at weekends and with whom Sam rarely socialised. Their only daughter joined the armed forces and has never visited home. He was a caring father and cannot fathom his daughter's lack of contact.

He hates the urban changes brought about by migrants from Asia and the Middle East. Thai massage parlours, Turkish takeaways, Lebanese restaurants, Indian doctors, Korean dry cleaners and Chinese newsagents all irritate Sam. He wonders what is becoming of his country. A visit to the local newsagent, where seemingly a new Asian face appears every week, always displeases. Going to his hospital's cardiac clinic as an outpatient also irritates. He loathes being 'stethoscoped' by foreign registrars. Sam has long suffered heart irregularities.

His closest friend and 60 year old bachelor neighbour, Tom, is terminally ill and Sam spends time visiting him at a nearby hospice. Before Tom took ill, Sam would encourage him to use dating services, claiming that Tom would enjoy a bit of fluff in his senior years. Tom would regularly help Sam with home maintenance in his old terrace house. He loved taking the micky out of Sam when he saw him doing household chores in his wife's old aprons. Tom and Sam are devoted to morning radio programs and both take delight when the shock jocks give it to the politicians. Neither has a mobile phone.

Strangely Tom's illness has not led Sam to ponder death. He was raised as a Baptist, attending Sunday school for a period. He accepts there is a god and has no fear about his final journey. His mother's old bible is in his bedside drawer. Tears are shed whenever he takes out from the bible an old photo which shows Tom as an 11 year old standing alongside his mother. His mother was a great cook. He missed her cakes and puddings. A sore point with his wife was that she never bothered cooking these treats.

Sam loves rugby league and cannot wait for Autumn to come around when he dotes on league news and the TV broadcasts. He used to go to games of his beloved Roosters but finds travel and crowds an annoyance. Summertime is loathed because of the humidity. Tom helped him to install a portable air conditioner in his living room and a ceiling fan in his bedroom.

Sam's gets great joy visiting the harbour, taking ferry trips on bright clear winter days. He now visits Cockatoo Island, meandering around the old sites and thinking about ship building there in the 19th century. He never studied Australian history and, not being a reader, has little knowledge of convict history of the island.

Attacks and rallies by various protest groups on the Australian identity and symbols rile Sam. He cannot understand the apparent dislike people have for Australian values and icons. He fumes over protest groups who want to change the flag, the anthem and the symbols of British heritage. As his own quiet protest, Sam has mounted an Australian flag on his upstairs balcony. He loves to see opposition to these protest rallies. He regularly tells Tom that he despises political activists who disapprove of his Australia.

There are not many personal matters that worry Sam. He fears that his pub may close, as he sees other local pubs sold up and turned into commercial offices and shops. At one stage Sam thought that male barber shops were going to disappear when his old barber shop closed and was replaced by a unisex hair dressing salon which he disliked. However, a new men's barber has started up locally which he is patronising. Initially he was troubled by female bus drivers but now has adjusted to their presence.

He knows he has to arrange for Tom's funeral when he passes. Tom has no relatives. He cannot broach the topic of funerals with Tom when he visits. Tom somehow believes that he will recover and refuses to believe that an ending is imminent. Sam has not explored the options for his own funeral.

Sam cannot muster the will to reach out to his daughter. He continually ponders what has occurred to bring this break in relationship and communication. After all, he was a devoted father leaving discipline to his wife. Wherever appropriate he would support his daughter in her school and sporting activities, giving all the affection of a proud father.

The current state of politics gets fleeting attention whenever Sam reflects about the social and economic conditions around him. All political parties appear to wrestle with the same agendas and he rarely follows their political debates in the media. At the local level, however, he admires his local councillor who has fought to keep the ferry maintenance depot at its original site, as well as ensuring that street parking is prioritised for local residents.

Sam never feels he is a loner nor feels lonesome. He draws comfort in his daily activities and with his nodding acquaintanceship with neighbours. As he encounters change, social and technological, he feels comforted by the routines of his life which shield him.

Sam is happy that his final days will be spent in his Inner West neighbourhood.

Tara

Most weekdays Tara takes her small hairy terrier for a harbourside walk. She prefers mid mornings when suburban activity has slowed. Initially she was a reluctant dog walker but now values her outing with the dog. It gets her away from home, giving her the opportunity to interact with other walkers, who have become an important part of her social network. The dog was purchased at the insistence of her two school-aged children who now have little interest nor time for the dog's care and well-being. She discreetly carries black plastic bags used to dispose of dog poo.

Tara is willowy slender and has her brown hair closely cropped exposing her longish ear lobes, is 178 centimetres tall and towers over her husband. She ensures she is neatly attired for her walks, favouring slacks, vests of bright colours and occasionally colourful bandanas. At 32 years old she feels proud that she has kept her figure trim. She would love to walk faster but the dog cannot keep pace. Her large size feet mean she has often trouble getting walking shoes to match her colour preferences.

Unlike other mothers in her street she has not returned to work, preferring to support the children while they are at primary school. She is casual with household chores and tends to do her cleaning and laundry at the last minute.

Households around her employ cleaners. She would like to update their household appliances but being a single-income family places limits on the household budget. Vet fees for the dog, which requires frequent treatment, challenge budget management.

A strong friendship network, developed through school functions and former work colleagues, keeps Tara socially active. Her husband is regularly interstate with work. He tolerates Tara's friends and attends school functions and dinner parties reluctantly. An unadventurous cook, Tara rarely entertains at home and dinners are supplemented by dishes prepared elsewhere.

Tara worries about her looks and goes to great lengths to ensure she keeps up with cosmetic trends and clothing fashions. She constantly checks her slight jowl and wonders whether it will worsen with age. Freddie, her local gay hairdresser, charms her, and in his strange flirtatious way causes her to think she is an attractive woman. Her Facebook entries cause her to flinch at her face which she feels is too long and pinched.

Her normally positive outlook is undermined by her forty year old husband whose ardour in the bedroom has waned dramatically. He rarely comments on the children's attainments and her involvements. He spends no time with the dog and avoids home maintenance. However, in all other respects, he is caring and helpful when prompted. She suspects he is having an affair but does not dare enquire, keeping her concerns to herself. Her parents' divorce, when she was a teenager, reminds her of the fragility of marriage and partnerships. Some of her friends and fellow dog walkers are either remarried or are between relationships.

Both her parents enjoy their grandchildren, and her mother, who visits regularly, will often take the children for weekend and holiday breaks. Her father is an occasional visitor. She fails to get her husband to have a night away with her in a friend's Blue Mountains house in these breaks. This tends to confirm her suspicion about her husband's infidelity.

Tara has become the social secretary for her two small friendship circles - one from her school and university days, the other with women she has met at the children's school. She loves to sample new economical eateries, arranging get togethers once every six or seven weeks. She treasures these outings because she finds that they help her to maintain confidence and shed uncertainties, which her husband has generated through his indifference. The conversations always surprise her, especially the frankness in dealing with personal lives and health concerns. What she regrets is that the high she experiences during these occasions is often deflated by the boorish behaviour of her husband who seemingly resents her enjoyment.

Many of her friends have encouraged her to return to work as a marketing analyst. This skill was gained in the pharmaceutical industry. Her concern for her children puts a brake on this for the foreseeable future. However, her skills have been kept sharp through analysis work to support local activist groups campaigning for more open space and community amenities in former industrial sites.

Walking the dog has become good therapy for Tara, especially when visiting the harbour- side parks. She is able to ponder and work through issues without being cluttered with domestic and interpersonal matters. She contemplates the challenges of returning to work, the options of secondary schooling for the children, possible conversations about marital relations with her husband and the wisdom of changing careers when she returns to work. Political debates and controversies, which some of her friends get excited about, do not interest her. The only hazard she has encountered with dog walking is occasional abuse of park users who resent dogs in the parks. Once, an elderly man hurled abuse by calling her terrier a mobile shit machine.

She remains confident that whatever unfolds in her marriage and future work she will succeed, having inherited her mother's assuredness and spirit of adventure. And what continues to puzzle her is the number of prominent women in the arts and politics who believe inequality bedevils the lot of women. Sexism and discrimination, when studying and working, were never encountered. She also reflects whether amongst her friendship circle it is unusual not to have encountered gay people.

Tara wonders how long her terrier, now approaching nine years, will live. She has resolved that she will buy another when he dies. In her mind dog walking is very therapeutic.

Luke

On non-childcare days, usually two days a week, house dad Luke regularly spends an hour or so with his three year old son at a nearby café, where he enjoys a large latte. He relishes this break since a waitress normally diverts his son while Luke is busy with his mobile. Luke is oblivious to the disturbance his son causes when he runs amok around customers at their tables. The waitress, a young Asian lady, tries to corral the boy with bribes of baby chinos and marshmallows. Customers look disapprovingly at Luke when his mobile consumes his attention.

Luke is tall, slightly podgy, bespectacled and covers his thinning hair with a Nike cap which is rarely removed when he visits the café. He sometimes is unshaven, which accentuates his brooding face, a perpetual scowl and unkemptness. He always wears faded jeans and one of his Ralph Lauren polo shirts which has seen better days. The unruly son wears kids-designer tops with his jeans. In summer both wear thongs. The son's unruly behaviour has extended to supermarket trips, when the son has tantrums if demands for a treat are not met.

Luke

Apart from the waitress, Luke does not acknowledge other customers. He has an air of arrogance and appears disdainful of the older customers. When Luke celebrated his thirty sixth birthday a waitress gave him a complimentary muffin to celebrate the occasion. A reluctant mumble accompanied his thanks.

Luke became the home parent following his wife becoming a partner in a boutique law firm. Her salary was three times the amount he was earning. They decided they would be a one child family. Luke intends to return to work when his son starts school. He is not certain whether he will return to work as a sales representative for a large wine distributor. His wife of nine years was met at a wine promotion event at a law conference.

Their perpetually untidy terrace was bought two years ago and partly financed by his wife's parents. The refurbished terrace was his wife's selection. He had little input in the decision. They have a house cleaner who comes every Monday and alternate Thursdays to handle the usual backlog of laundry and ironing. The cleaner used to come on Fridays only but the disorder and debris generated at weekends forced a change in arrangements.

The mobile has been Luke's pipeline to sanity. He maintains a network of male friends whom he calls most weeks. The comradeship of his mates is sorely missed. Evening meals are rarely prepared; takeaways have been the main fare which his wife brings on her way home. It is rare that she is home before 7pm. On weekends pizzas and takeaway chicken feature regularly at the dinner table.

Intimate moments are infrequent, occurring usually on Saturday nights. His wife is often too distracted or on edge during the working week for romantic interludes. As well their son often refuses to sleep alone and shares their bed.

Luke is not happy with this and feels he is being sidelined. Privately he lusts after a neighbour who lives three doors up the street. The 41 year old divorcee works locally as a real estate agent. He marvels at her impeccable taste in clothes and svelteness and is envious of her flash new Audi. Luke drives an old Mazda whilst his wife drives a leased BMW sedan.

Luke and his wife rarely see or hear from their parents, who all live in Victoria. He does not miss contact, although it would be nice for their son to spend time with them. They are relieved that they have a neighbour's daughter to help with babysitting.

The time Luke best enjoys with his wife is on their annual holiday. Before and after their son's birth they holidayed at one of the Pacific islands for a two week stay. Noumea, Vanuatu and Fiji have been visited, but since the arrival of their son they have been to Fiji where they find child care services have been a real bonus. Increasingly though he has noticed his wife finds it difficult to unwind and to forget her professional work. He diverts himself by patronising the resort bars and chatting with resort staff.

Luke resents that he can rarely join his former work associates for occasional Friday lunch or evening pub gatherings. His wife will not take days off or work from home. In a way he feels trapped. Many Fridays she is rarely home before 7pm because of social commitments at work. He used to join his wife at stifling work functions but found them boring and felt he was a wallflower. He now declines invites to outings with her colleagues, preferring to stay home and watch DVDs.

While returning to sales representative work is a possibility, he hopes he can find a new direction when he gives up house parenting. He fears that he is losing his old networks and contacts and wonders whether his absence from commerce will impede his chances of getting back into the fray of competitive work. His technology skills have not kept pace with new developments. Industry has also changed dramatically especially the promotion and marketing of wine. Former work contacts have moved on after new ownerships brought about changes in wine logistics and distribution.

Some male neighbours have taken up weekend bike riding and invited Luke to join them. Initially he thought he would do so but then considered that the exercise value was overstated and he did not see himself as too flash in a Lycra outfit. His wife thought the idea as laughable, given Luke's history of being totally inept at sport. She had also mocked Luke about his intention to get a sports tattoo on his right shoulder.

The changes in his neighbourhood have interested Luke. He sees more young families moving in and the older residents moving out. He notes that there is a sprinkle of house dads popping up in parks and the supermarket. And at the child care centre, the number of fathers dropping off and picking up kids has certainly increased. He has shied away from befriending them. He feels that he has nothing in common with them and does not want any more exposure to and conversations about the trials and tribulations of house parenting.

The political discussions his wife raises incessantly annoy Luke. She remains a staunch Labor Party supporter but has not maintained her membership. Luke does not care about the plight of the unemployed, the aborigines, the down trodden, the gender benders and refugees - topics which his wife regularly discusses. There is also little sympathy for wastrels, believing that all able adults must be more personally responsible for their destinies and independently remedy their problems.

Luke will see out home parenting commitments in order to keep his partnership workable whilst tolerating irritant home arrangements.

Prue

Keeping fit is now an obsession with Prue. Since her separation three years ago, the 49 year old hairdresser has maintained a strict exercise regime which includes a twice weekly session of Pilates at a local gym. Her instructor compliments Prue on her commitment to fitness and health and her desire to excel at the routines. Of medium height, she keeps her angular body in good shape but does, when viewing herself in a mirror, flinch at her elongated face, long torso, small bust and shortish legs. She believes regular exercise will mitigate the effects of menopause.

Prue normally wears her exercise clothes when walking to the gym, with usually a jacket over her Lycra outfit. Her habit is to carry her personal exercise mat under her arm rather than in a sling across her back. Prue prefers to be bareheaded and only wears hats in summer - ones that she bought from the Cancer Council. Her only annoyance with Pilates is the behaviour of two fellow exercisers who are apt to be exhibitionists.

As part of her health regime she avoids caffeine and meat eating, and where possible prefers organic fruit and vegetables. She is relieved that she does not need to cook meat for her high school son, her only child, who is a full-time boarder at a private school in Armidale, and mostly stays with his father in the holidays. Her health campaign includes dabbling in naturopathy and seeking acupuncture treatment for any joint pains.

There is little contact with her husband who lives on the northern beaches. Their separation was amicable. Divergent lifestyles drove them apart. Her partner spent a lot of time on golf and fishing trips. Once their son went to boarding school, it became apparent that they had little in common. He could not tolerate any of her food and health preferences. Divorce proceedings are underway.

Prue now works part-time and is on call as a hairdresser. Until recently she managed a salon but found the pressures too much. She had entertained the idea of working on cruise ships, but lost interest when she realised the downside of confining ship-board life. She prefers working for female managers, finding many male managers too overbearing and over critical of her styling skills.

Her best friend Angela, also a hairdresser and separated, is a regular companion and they share a love of romantic movies. They meet once or twice a month and have gone on vacations together especially to Bali and Phuket where they can afford hotels and restaurants. Both ladies once or twice fancied the idea of 'cougaring' themselves when abroad. But they always went cold on the idea, preferring to keep a distance from male company when overseas. Prue however would like to meet a male for long-term companionship, believing that her becalmed libido could be activated if the right man came along.

Angela reminds Prue that her lifestyle and outlook limit the choice of male partners. Prue is a strong advocate of the Green agenda and is not shy of arguing her position about pollution, deteriorating public services and the economic forces destroying community life. In recent times she has joined a small advocacy group to pressure for more overnight shelters for the homeless and abused. Cases of the less fortunate appearing on TV upset her.

Her elderly parents live on the Central Coast at Mc Masters Beach, where she makes it a habit to visit every three or four weeks. Her married sister in Townsville is in contact and they join their parents for most Christmas celebrations. Her son spends part of January with her parents. Prue loves to swim in summer which triggers thoughts about her physique and whether she should consider cosmetic surgery to enhance her bust line.

Blessed by friendly neighbours, Prue enjoys her apartment with its distant views of Sydney's skyline. The small apartment complex houses retirees, working singles and couples. She enjoys a good rapport with the residents, who hold the odd evening cocktail gathering, especially in summer. They marvel at Prue's commitment to exercise. One of the male neighbours jokes about her striding along the streets carrying her Pilates paraphernalia and has remarked that Prue could be viewed as running a mobile bordello with her exercise mat used as bedding. Strangely she feels this as a compliment. After all, she is getting older and not endowed with the figure normally associated with female escorts.

Apartment living suits Prue. When her divorce is concluded she will be able to buy an annuity to support herself well into the future. The only nuisance she encounters in the apartment is with her upstairs neighbour, a retired lady, who over waters plants on her balcony which spills down over her balcony. To date she has not summoned up the courage to complain. Whilst not a serious irritant, she can't stand the smell of barbecued meat wafting up from the complex's barbecue area.

Prue has considered moving to the far North Coast once her divorce is finalised. Her thoughts were that a new location and community might bring new friendships and even perhaps romance. She has a number of coastal towns on her short list and has a long-held desire to get into a coastal environment well away from the pollution and noise of urban living. Both her parents and Angela have urged Prue to think through the pros and cons of moving, because there is evidence that pioneering a new life distant from her colleagues and family might not turn out to be a bed of roses.

A new venture for Prue has been to join an informal lady's gymnastic group. She enjoys the work outs with other women in her age group. The exercise has improved her muscle tone and aerobic condition. As well, she finds it generates a calm and positive temperament.

Sifting through personal health improvement recommendations in a host of health guides and TV programs has not always been helpful to Prue. She has difficulty discerning the scientific basis of these and tends to rely on her intuition to decide on any changes in her diet and exercise. She remains ambivalent about the ethical basis of some of the health supplements promoted through magazine and media programs.

Prue's life is approaching a pivotal point. She has choices to make but she is comforted by the fact she remains healthy and active.

Wendy

Sundays cannot come fast enough for 76 year old diminutive spinster Wendy. She loves her church, its rituals, solemnity and predictability. The world of upheaval has been kept at bay. Wendy cherishes the constancy and traditions experienced in her church. Conservative sermons together with classic hymns and music give Wendy immense pleasure. She is pleased that the changes in ministers over time have not disturbed the well-established conventions of the church and is ambivalent about a future minister being a female. No matter what occurs in her daily life, the prospect of Sunday church is always a beacon of joy.

The evening before church Wendy reviews her wardrobe and has stuck to selecting four outfits which she rotates. In winter she will wear a light overcoat. She always matches her shoes with muted coloured outfits of blouses and skirts or dresses. She rarely wears a hat and keeps her fine grey hair traditionally styled which suits her fair complexion. Her jewellery is normally a necklace or brooch, both of which she inherited from her mother. Wendy is conscious of her posture and keeps her body as upright as possible when walking and sitting. Of late her skin seems paper-thin and notes she bruises easily whenever she has a bump or knock.

For the last eight years Wendy has lived in a retirement village, where she is able to garage her small Nissan saloon which she uses for shopping, medical visits, church and the odd outing. Both her parents are buried at Narromine, which was her home town before she left at the age of 16 to take a job with the Bank of NSW. Before she acquired the unit in the village, Wendy lived alone for most of her working life in a small group of flats. The village has an exercise program which she follows to keep her 49 kilo body fit.

A former workmate, Lorraine, is her closest friend. They meet and socialise regularly, attending music concerts, galleries and the NSW Art Gallery where they reminisce in its cafe about their jobs and their former work colleagues. They both are monarchists and love to read about the royal family. Politics is always another conversation piece and is fuelled by the trials and tribulations of the Liberal Party which they have always supported. They had mixed feelings about gay marriage but this is now no longer a topic of conversation.

Wendy never feels lonely. She has amicable relations with other village residents, joining social functions when the mood takes her. A lot of her enjoyment comes from cooking, especially cakes and slices for church functions. Consuming a glass of white wine with her evening meals has become normal over the past 12 years, following introduction and encouragement from Lorraine when dining together. Verdelho is her favourite. Whilst she enjoys TV, most of her pleasure comes from listening to classical music and reading about church news. She has never travelled abroad and takes vacations with Lorraine. Of late they have been journeying around southern Australia on bus tours.

Occasionally she reflects about why, when younger, she had no strong urge to seek male company and to consider the prospect of marriage and children. Life was sheltered on her parents' rural property and male schoolfriends did not attract her interest. An old aunt used to jibe her about being left on the shelf but she found that farm work, visiting cousins, reading and church-going gave her a teenage life with which she was comfortable. While she went on several late adolescent dates, she never experienced the romantic desires and urges mentioned by her girlfriends.

The viability of her church and its dwindling, aging congregation frequently haunt her thoughts. Around her nearby suburbs she notes that some churches have been sold or rebranded to another denomination sometimes under the control of ethnic groups usually from Asia or the Pacific. No matter how long she ponders this decline in church attendance she is not able to come up with sound ideas to attract new members. Her church has employed a number of schemes and activities to attract new members but they always fail to yield an enduring increase in attendance. The small boost in attendance at Easter and Christmas never converts to an ongoing larger congregation.

Wendy does not dwell on health issues which seem to be an endless discussion topic in her village. Doctors would go bankrupt if they had patients like Wendy. She self-medicates for the normal aches and pains. There has been no medical trauma in her life apart from a broken wrist at home and a broken collar bone from an accident at work. A vitamin sceptic she visits her local doctor rarely and then only for the usual check-ups, annual flu shot and fitness to drive assessment.

Maintaining an open mind on cultural, political and economic issues is something Wendy holds dear when they arise in her social encounters. She is always attracted by logical and rational arguments, although she gets unsettled by debates about religious dogma. All the changes evident from multicultural Australia are considered positive. Intolerance and racism are real evils in Wendy's eyes. And she has deep sympathy for the plight of indigenous communities and their pursuit of rights and recognition.

Sometimes Wendy thinks about death and has already organised for her remains to be placed alongside her parents. Often these days she thinks of the wording for her epitaph. While she favours a biblical inscription on her memorial plaque, she is mindful that something contemporary has appeal. Her father had on his memorial the words of the song writer Irving Berlin "The song has ended but the melody lingers on". She has insured for her funeral expenses. A local solicitor will execute her will, dividing her estate between her church and a women's refuge association.

Whatever holds for Wendy's future she draws continuing comfort from her faith and the knowledge that her encounters in life never caused harm to others. There is no regret about the pathway she has chosen.

Aileen

~ ZEALOUS ADVOCATE ~

Rallies, protests, petitions, demonstrations, sit-ins, campaigns, marches, letters to editors, parades, boycotts, occupations, road blocks and convoys are all part of Aileen's dissent repertoire. She is the consummate activist and rights campaigner. At the age of 57, the heavyset and dowdy Aileen loves to take on a cause and to rattle her opponents. A relentless committee member, she is always ready to take up the gauntlet righting injustice, neglect, or inequity. At meetings, Aileen is always seated in the front row introducing herself to the meeting chairperson before proceedings commence. In some campaign circles, Aileen has been nicknamed, 'the protestess'.

The former librarian, retrenched four years ago, is long-divorced and is a devoted cat lover. Fashion and modern attire do not interest Aileen, who prefers loose fitting plain dresses and comfortable wide-fit half-boots. In summer her nod to fashion is her ever-present Nike walking sandals which accommodate her abnormal toe alignment. She never wears jewellery. Her long hair is tidied with either a bun or a florid motif headband which she believes compliments her sallow complexion and fleshy face. Enlivening her largely drab attire is one of her colourful shoulder satchels, which contain personal items. She is never seen with a handbag.

AILEEN

Present causes gaining her attention include refugees, animal rights, the homeless, renewable energy, public transport and prisoner reform. To advance impact, Aileen builds networks with like-minded advocates. Current phone numbers of local parliamentarians, councillors, government agencies and advocate groups are stored on her phone. Her tenant, a younger woman working in computer software, assists Aileen occasionally with building websites for the causes she is prosecuting. She patiently suffers Aileen's rants and earbashing whenever a crusade is in play.

Her four - bedroom terrace is forever cluttered with books, pamphlets and placards. The dusty décor has remained unchanged over the 22 year period of Aileen's ownership. The only photo in her bedroom is that of her elderly widowed father who lives in Newtown. Aileen never mentions her husband although she has told her tenant that it was a loveless marriage without children. There is friction with her neighbours, who have objected both to her and the local council about the unsightly placards placed along her front fence for the cause of the moment. The odd noisy fund -raising function, which has breached noise level regulations, also generates friction.

Fellow campaigners regard Aileen as a generous good-hearted person. When socialising her hypochondria wears the patience of some, whenever her current malady overwhelms conversations. Arthritis together with long-term blood circulation and dermatological issues become regular conversation topics. The local pathology service, pharmacy and medical centre are beneficiaries of Aileen's ailments.

Aileen donates generously to charities. Her income from her late mother's trust and work pension enable her to enjoy a comfortable lifestyle, to take vacations and to support refugee housing and welfare. What miffs Aileen is that she has never received a direct personal thank you or expression of gratitude from the refugees she has supported. Privately she wonders whether this is a cultural issue or her support is regarded by them as a sort of presumptive right for the ill treatment they received from authorities. This lack of appreciation has baffled her. Aileen never offers to house refugees even though her friends have requested it on a number of occasions. To avoid her embarrassment on this she responds that the space is required for her tenant.

Taking her campaigns to high schools has been an important objective. Rebuffs from principals have angered Aileen. They argue there is too much of a political tinge in her proposed presentations. She has found that the best way to approach students is to give them a campaign cap whenever they are present at protest gatherings. Apathy and disinterest among adults are continuing challenges to generating support, especially when there are calls for attendance at public rallies.

Aileen is aligned with the Greens on most policies except for schools. Education received in Catholic schools is considered by Aileen a key to raising the social conscience of a population. Aileen enjoyed a Catholic education and is a relentless advocate for church schools. Up till four years ago she attended mass regularly. Always devout, the scandalous events in the church have unsettled her. Mass attendance has become sporadic following the appointment of an annoying Croatian priest, whose thick accent cripples the presentation of the service.

Contempt and disdain are what Aileen holds for those politicians who are incapable of avowing and then upholding principles and values to direct their actions. They often agree with her positions at meetings but fail to vote or act on the undertakings given. Many of her friends have helped her by resorting to social media to attack them for the lack of spine and principles. A problem in securing political support for her causes is that commercial radio commentators fail to respond to her pleas for action.

There was a time Aileen could persuade local shopkeepers to put her campaign posters in their shop fronts. This opportunity has disappeared. Many shops are empty. Supportive owners have been replaced by rental operators who refuse to display. Many cafes decline, not risking to offend their patrons. Apart from social media, letter box drops retain their importance for promoting a cause.

Friends find there is an inner Aileen that remains unrevealed, despite her social persona, frankness and openness on such matters as personal health. At times she appears to have a sadness and at other times a deep melancholy is evident. Aileen keeps her relationship bruises withheld. Her marriage was marred by dispute as well as a fruitless, frustrated, and mechanically fulfilled sexually intimacy. She wonders whether her sensuality was curbed by religious dictates and genital apprehension. She is disconcerted that close friendships at school, college, work and elsewhere have eluded her. Her congeniality masks a lack of confidence and preparedness to share with others her deep personal feelings and fears. Such sharing can build friendships and cement closer relationships. A private unhappiness has endured.

There is always a social cause or injustice attracting Aileen's notice. These will bring her on to the protest stage, diverting thoughts of unhappiness and the absence of close friendships.

Colin

Most mornings around 7 am. Colin, or Col to his friends, makes his way to his local café with his faithful hound Bett, or Bettany to Col's local vet, to have his mug of flat white. They command an outside table or, in bad weather, Col will tether Bett outside under the awning cover and sit inside. There are five or so regulars whom Colin greets as long- term friends. He finds the chat and companionship of early coffee mornings give him a sense of belonging, following his wife's placement in care two years ago. She long suffered dementia.

Good health and fitness, sound hearing and eyesight enable the lean, tall 78 year old to remain independent at home. He was a devoted carer and now regularly visits his wife at her care residence. A great marriage, three happily married offspring together with eight grandchildren, comfort Colin in his quieter moments. The family visit his wife once or twice a month, usually at weekends. Both mobile and internet technology do not faze Colin, yet he prefers to link up with his family with phone calls. Knowing their father abhors texting, all his children will phone home on a regular basis. Colin never takes his mobile on his café visits.

The 16 years of retirement have not troubled him. The skills he acquired as a master toolmaker have been put to good use around the home. He renovated a kitchen and built a glass house where he cultivates orchids - now a consuming passion. His neighbours are envious of his home maintenance prowess. Colin has fixed most broken appliances, painted his cottage twice, refenced the whole backyard and services his Holden Commodore, which has been kept in pristine order. He is a legend both at the café, where he has corrected faults in the coffee machinery, and with neighbours, when he resolves their house maintenance problems.

Interacting with his fellow workers was always a positive for Colin. Many of his older work colleagues imparted new skills and insights which Colin gratefully received. He likewise was always eager to assist others at work, especially apprentices with whom he had successful mentoring relationships. Retirement reunion lunches are enjoyed by Colin. His link with his former job, apart from the pension fund, is his work overalls which he wears on jobs around the house. On retirement he was given 20 new pairs of superseded overalls carrying his employer's former logo.

Café regulars like Colin. His open, cheery and courteous character brightens up the morning. A good listener, a valuable sounding board and a wealth of practical knowledge, he is a popular regular among the assortment of mostly single householders and flat dwellers gathered for their morning caffeine fix. When there are quiet times Colin will read the newspapers, skipping the political news, preferring the sports pages and news items relating to local events. Avoiding political issues at the café and home has been Colin's approach when he gets into discussions. He keeps his own counsel on politics.

Unsettling the general calmness of Colin are the rantings by social commentators and leaders who make him silently fume. He finds it all too much. He vents his concerns to his children and his atheist neighbour, Vince. Colin believes there is a greater power or force in the universe, but that is as far he is prepared to accept. He is a regular donor to charities run by St Vincent de Paul and the Salvation Army.

He believes Australia is a great country and becomes concerned when various groups question its customs and values. Australia gives all a fair go and countless opportunities for a healthy, secure and happy life. His grandparents were British migrants who, from scratch, built a successful life in Australia. He is proud of multicultural achievements in Australia and enjoys the diversity of food and life styles introduced.

For a while Colin played bowls until his wife sickness required intensive care. The fraternity bowls generated compensated Colin for loss of work friendships which he cherished. While many raise questions about the depth and emotional sincerity of mateship, Colin finds it critical to keep a balanced sense of life and explains, in his own mind, the importance of coffee mornings with its potential to bring more vitality into his life.

Orchid cultivation has provided a great form of relaxation as well as a link to a whole community of orchid fanciers. The detail and investigation accompanying orchid growing match Colin's organising and planning disposition. The prospect of a two- week group tour of New Zealand's orchid producers is exciting Colin, requiring him to think how he can explain his absence to his wife and whether it will create a negative emotional reaction. He has already contacted another tour member who is prepared to share accommodation. A map of New Zealand on his bedside table is studied from time to time.

Shopping does not irritate Colin except when his supermarket rearranges its shelves and disturbs his routine aisle movement. He buys most of his clothes at a popular menswear store, outfitting himself conventionally and rarely departing from black, grey and blue shades in colour. A main concession to modernity was the purchase of 'Crocs' which he regards as the perfect casual footwear at home. Colin is never seen in thongs which he regards as hazardous footwear. A real frustration in clothing arises from his underwear which do not have a conventional fly. 'Unflied' undies he calls them. He feels obliged to wear them because they were birthday gifts. He hates visiting public urinals when wearing them because he imagines fellow 'urinators' smirking as he struggles to release his appendage from his 'sealed' underwear and tucked-in shirt.

Since his wife has been in care, Colin has been taking Bett for long walks around a nearby cove. When unleashed Bett will head for the water for a gambol. Talking to Bett has been strangely comforting, something he never did when his wife was present. He notices some of his fellow coffee drinkers are often talking to their dogs. What is the psychological benefit of such discourse he reflects? Does it offset loneliness, does it strengthen the relationship with the dog, or does it indicate an innate need to express care and love? All these often pass through Colin's mind on his cove perambulations.

Eating well has always been Colin's concern. His wife prepared lovely evening meals and Sunday lunches which he has missed. Trying ready- prepared meals from the supermarket disappointed, because they were inevitably gluggy, tasteless or too greasy. Cooking for himself never gave much satisfaction and he could not match his wife's standards. By chance he found a local shop preparing hot meals which occasionally has been his salvation. On some weekends his children invite him over for dinner.

Colin sees his life being presented with positive experiences. Visits to his wife remind him that he is blessed to have good health and there is always good amongst his fellow Australians.

Paul

~ CHALLENGED PARENT ~

School day mornings are not welcomed by 33 year old dentist Paul. They are always testing times as he organises his five year old daughter to prepare for school. Retrieving her uniform from the laundered pile, serving breakfast, preparing the school lunch and shepherding her out the house are the least of his challenges. Encouraging and ushering a reluctant and often crying daughter along the road to the local school test Paul's patience. He cajoles, bribes and urges to get her to the school gate, where fortunately a duty teacher takes over. He drops her off by 8.30 and collects her at 5.30 from the home of another parent who is paid for after-school care. Paul arrives at his clinic often on edge and exhausted.

The slightly built, flat-footed, bulgy-eyed, pinched-faced dentist does not enjoy his profession. Paul wanted to study architecture but his dominating father insisted that he do dentistry, which was a family tradition. His father paid all the university fees. Paul's passage through his degree was a struggle and not helped by his nervous and shy disposition, compounded by a mournful face and a slight stoop. He found dental training a chore. Since graduation he found it difficult to get regular employment because his employers found that Paul's marginal skills, together with his off-putting personality and indifference, real handicaps.

Paul

Presently Paul works four days a week in a large clinic, where usually he is assigned elderly patients. Other dentists in the practice do not hold him in high regard.

Marriage has not been kind to Paul. His wife, formerly a dental receptionist, now operates a disability care service which leaves her little leisure time. Paul finds their relationship stressful. Following the birth of their daughter his wife retrained as a care worker and now runs her own business, which she plans to expand over the next two years. Home management and most chores are left to Paul. Her busy schedule, involving six days a week, leaves Paul to undertake the care and support of their daughter. A cleaner comes once a fortnight to help out. Compounding their relationship is Paul being unable to deal with his wife's demands and directions. His retiring and hesitant disposition is no match for her dominant and overbearing personality. Paul avoids disputes and capitulates when differences arise.

To colleagues and friends Paul appears as a dreamy character, lacking real drive and a sense of purpose. Privately Paul harbours the desire to become a designer, but cannot see how he could pursue this financially as well as countering his wife's opposition to abandoning dentistry. His dentistry work is critical in supporting their mortgage, whilst her care business is being developed. Paul wishes that he had someone close with whom he could discuss his frustrations and ambitions.

Opportunities to escape the burdens of work and child rearing are limited, leaving Paul little time for himself. Wherever possible and where the appointment schedule permits, Paul will take himself for a walk to the harbour - his sanctuary. Of late he is letting things at work get him down. His pet hates are patients with halitosis and ulcerated gums. He angered the practice manager by insisting that some patients with serious halitosis go to their medico first before he starts treatment. He rarely has coffee or lunch with the other dentists in the practice.

Handling his daughter constantly challenges Paul. He believes that the daughter's erratic and obstinate behaviour can be attributed to her resenting the absence and inattention of her mother. In a way he feels she is reacting to her mother's indifference and coldness. Twice a week he takes his daughter to dance lessons which have become a continuing hassle. There are tantrums to manage before class and as well when she refuses to eat the evening meal, which he normally prepares. Even when his wife joins them, her refusals and grumpiness can still be nerve-wracking. Neither Paul's nor his wife's parents are able to assist with child rearing, since they are all busy running businesses.

Close friendships have eluded Paul since high school. Two high school friends have moved interstate and contact is rare. He has good relations with his neighbours. He occasionally will attend AFL matches with his older brother whenever they are held on Sundays. There are limited chances for Paul to build new friendships. He would like to undertake some evening art classes but he cannot see any possibility with the business commitments of his wife. Paul considers talking with his wife about getting some personal time to himself but backs out when he contemplates her likely hostile reaction.

Reading is Paul's favoured leisure activity. His current interests are biographies of artists and books on interior design. Newspapers do not excite him but he spends time reading the review section in the Saturday Australian on Sundays whenever his wife takes the daughter to the shops or visits her parents. Occasionally during quiet times, Paul will sketch plants and houses which have striking features.

His sketchbook represents his yearnings for another pathway in life.

Troubling Paul is his working relationship with his colleagues who are cool towards him and he suspects they disparage his skills. Apart from the Xmas drinks and birthdays there is no socialising. He experiences a high turnover of dental nurses and rarely has he had the same nurse lasting more than two months. The owner has built a strong practice and Paul believes that he is there on sufferance and serious complaints might find him looking for another position. Despite urging from his wife to start his own practice he knows that this is not a genuine observation given his role at home supporting her business ambitions.

Since their marriage they have holidayed twice; once before their daughter was born and once when she was three. Both vacations were fraught with his wife's complaints about the restaurants and the quality of hotel services. She tended to find fault with even the most trivial matter, insisting that Paul lodge all the complaints and do the chasing up wherever she remained dissatisfied. For peace and harmony Paul yielded to his wife's demands.

Paul feels there are few positive elements in his life. He is attached to his daughter and has romantic feelings about his wife. A sense of fulfillment awaits. He is imprisoned by life's duties.

Harry

~ DEVOTED BROTHER ~

Most weekday mornings middle-aged casual market worker, Harry, travels out to a morning shift at his fruit vendor employer. Before dawn he leaves his flat, shared with his much younger invalid pensioner sister. Normally a carer comes in the mornings to support his sister. Harry occasionally joins other workers for a schooner or two at their local, before returning home early in the afternoon. It is now six years since their mother passed, when he took over caring responsibility for his sister, June.

Before taking on caring duties Harry worked as a roof tiler. His dark complexion, weathered face, sinewy physique and well-muscled arms indicate a life of heavy labour. A chronic barking cough tells a tale of a life time smoker. His shock of greying black hair and strong torso suggest a movie star quality, generating ribbings from fellow workers about his lady-killer potential.

The public housing unit he shares with his sister was also home to his late widowed mother. Their unit complex houses mostly elderly occupants. Harry, a confirmed bachelor, had a short romantic relationship with a spinster in a unit below, but it was called off when she demanded a more permanent arrangement.

Harry

While he enjoys the company of women and, despite many torrid romances in his younger days, Harry has never seen the value of marriage, despite persistent urgings from his mother to marry and settle down.

Most evening meals are prepared by Harry. Both he and his sister have conservative tastes. Three veg and meat appear most nights, although Harry has experimented with pasta dishes and the odd lamb curry. Gladys, a neighbour, sometimes brings in a cake, as well as Harry's favourite meat dish, meatloaf. A taxi-driver friend occasionally takes both of them to a weekend lunch at a local club, where they enjoy a baked dinner. The only break from routine occurs when an aunt comes to stay, allowing Harry to spend a week away with mates, usually fishing at Port Stephens.

Friends admire Harry for his devotion to his sister, never hearing a word of resentment or discontent about the constant call on his support and the loss of opportunity to pursue other interests. Harry, when asked about this, simply responds this is what he would expect if he found himself in his sister's situation. To assist his sister, a tutor is employed on a casual basis working with his sister to give her internet and data technology skills. Harry supports many fund-raising activities for the handicapped, always pestering work mates and neighbours for contributions. One of the female charity collectors, residing nearby, occasionally invites him over for an afternoon drink which is sometimes followed by a steamy romantic interlude.

Fellow unit dwellers often call on Harry to help fix malfunctioning appliances and to move furniture. Like Harry they are rusted on Labor Party supporters, although they are not paid-up members of the party. Most join Harry in his abhorrence of Labor's advocacy of same sex marriage. At times Harry feels that his local Labor MP is too patronising.

His drinking mates think the MP is masquerading as a Green party member. Harry hates ABC radio because he believes its broadcasts have little appeal or connection with the concerns of ordinary Australians.

The changes in urban life unsettle Harry. Traditional shops, pubs and vendors have closed or moved, generating a barren atmosphere along the shopping strips, although he has welcomed the growth of cafes, where social hubs are formed via a morning coffee. The cottages and terraces surrounding his unit complex are forever being transformed through extensions, cladding or renovations. He sees more trades people than residents when he walks home from his bus stop. In earlier times many residents would be outside gardening, gossiping or cleaning, offering a friendly hello or wave as he passed by. Newcomers seem too busy or detached to acknowledge long-time residents. His local pub, where locals use to gather for an evening or Saturday drink, has had a loss of patronage and is unlikely to survive. His sister, who spends a great deal of time sitting by her window, complains that the outside street scene has lost its interest as the colourful characters of early times have gradually evaporated.

Harry reflects about the changes in society. At the markets he encounters the best and worst of multi - cultural Australia. Depending on the encounter, he continually updates his impressions about the honesty and goodness of people, and notes that all ethnic groups have their good and bad apples. His cosmopolitan cohort supplies endless enjoyment through a seemingly boundless bonhomie.

Among fellow workers he finds the need to bond and share as strongly as he experienced when working as a tiler with Aussie mates. Among customers, rudeness and politeness cuts across all groups. Harry though loves his

Mediterranean workmates, who share his humour and banter about the shortcomings of Australians, especially politicians and sportsmen. Slowly he has seen changes in some of his Asian stall holders, particularly the Indians, who revel in the send ups and tomfoolery of workplace interactions. He loves sharing morning teas with his market friends who have introduced a great variety of exotic Asian and European snacks.

Honesty and fairness are principles inherited from his mother. He is observing that these principles are violated by hitherto trustworthy institutions. Churches, banks, unions, governments, universities, hospitals, insurance houses, charities are under question for their dishonest, deceptive or misleading behaviour. Harry is not naïve and understands that rottenness is not exclusive to the criminal class. The extent and pervasiveness of crooked behaviour is now a common topic between Harry and his friends.

At a personal level there is little worrying Harry as he considers retirement. He has no present or future financial stress through the small inheritance from his mother and his sister's social security. His casual work income, a retirement annuity together with public rental housing security underpin a secure future. A long-term personal concern for Harry is illness or death occurring and providing care for his sister. She is a nervy, fragile and shy person who has difficulty accepting strangers. Her technology tutor took weeks before there was ready acceptance. He is currently looking at options for supporting his sister when he is no longer around.

Healthwise Harry is free of any problems, although he knows a dentist 's visit is well overdue. A recent skin check by a specialist dermatologist found a nonthreatening basal cell carcinoma. Mates have urged him to have a prostate test which to date he has ignored.

Harry is a protector. His world brings him pleasure and provides time for providing the best possible brotherly guardianship and love.

Peta

A former actuary and now a full-time mother, Peta is an enthusiastic art student and loves the painting classes conducted in her local church hall. The opportunity to take classes came at a pivotal time when her two children were well settled at school and her daily household tasks reduced through work done by live-in overseas students participating in the 'woofer' program. The chance to pursue art, first introduced to her at high school, filled a long-term dream to become a landscape artist.

Peta gets a real buzz from preparing for her classes and completing her art assignments at home. Fashion conscious and keen to impress, she wears smart casuals to class ensuring they do justice to her tallish trim figure, her curly dark hair and rounded, sunny face. At home and at formal occasions, Peta draws compliments for her taste in clothes as well as in her colourful footwear, especially her high heel sandals. She is a compulsive toe-nail painter. Never self-conscious, Peta has always favoured revealing apparel when dressed for formal occasions. The 37 year old keeps her body in shape through sensible eating and regular exercise. The local organic food grocer enjoys her regular patronage.

Married for 12 years Peta has formed a strong and devoted partnership with her geologist husband. They are caring parents, ensuring their primary school sons have a well-rounded exposure to sports, music, and cultural events. They always enjoy an annual vacation together, preferring active vacations including skiing, bush walking and surfing. Extended families on both sides, with whom regular socialising occurs, add much to their happy life. Peta rarely argues with her husband who, in most years, spends two or three months away on field assignments skyping extensively to keep in touch with the family.

Landscape photos and colourful rock samples provided by her husband are used by Peta to build her micro and macro art skills. The art class sometimes share these as part of their object models. Peta senses a competitive tension in the class whenever the instructor offers comment on individual paintings in progress. Jealousy is not in Peta's make-up but she gets miffed whenever the instructor gives a superficial appraisal of her work. Some finished paintings hang in the professional offices of her husband. More development of her skills in landscape painting is planned when she can accompany her husband on his outback trips.

Peta considers that life has dealt her a good hand despite an early romantic set back. At university she became engaged to a fellow actuarial student in their final year of study. They planned to travel to London to work for a period. Relationships began to sour when her fiancé declared that he didn't want to have children. They broke up and a year later Peta met her husband on a vacation in Hawaii. They married a year later and settled in Balmain in a large terrace left to her husband by a grandparent.

Actuarial work and university allowed Peta to gain new friendships, introducing her to Asian lifestyles and cultures. Her now closest female friend, an unmarried Malaysian-Indian work colleague, opened up a whole new world of tastes and colours. Peta allowed herself to be bombarded by the sensory infusions of food, art, music and fabrics. They have an intense friendship, offering each other sounding boards to develop understanding of the emotional roller coaster of adult life. Peta has tried unsuccessfully to introduce her friend, who is not tied by cultural constraints, to male acquaintances with the possibility of longer-term relationship. Peta is saddened that her friend has, to date, not developed close male relationships.

Social responsibility has always underpinned Peta's approach to life. Ever conscious of the less fortunate, Peta volunteers in charity work and related fundraising activities. Elderly neighbours enjoy Peta's caring disposition. She assists, when needed, with transport to medical centres and shopping malls. One of her elderly neighbours, an artist, regularly visits to exchange views on Peta's work as well as accompanying her to exhibitions at local galleries.

Road rage is generating some grief whenever Peta is driving the family's large SUV. She has been the target of other drivers' abuse especially when she travels the local narrow urban streets. The tenor of the abuse is her road hogging and the obscenity of driving such a vehicle in restricted road ways. Peta ignores the verbal assaults but thinks perhaps there is some basis for the anger about vehicle size. In the past three years she has had to replace damaged wing mirrors caused by scraping parked vehicles.

While she has no intention to return to work as an actuary, she still receives job offers from her former employer. Work did provide a substantial income boost in her early married days, enabling Peta to build an extensive fashion wardrobe. Her desire to be fashionably dressed has not diminished. Local pop-up ladies fashion shops, which she combs assiduously for off-beat but stylish clothing, are well patronised. She still visits her former hairdresser, close to her old work place, to style her hair to match the trends of the modern working professional.

Ever confident about the security of her marriage and the prospects of her children, Peta's one hidden ambition is to achieve recognition of her artistic ability to match the praise and respect she achieved as an actuary. Her artist father, a finalist in a national art award, has been a silent driver of her ambition to do well in art. Supportive and loving, in his fatherly way, he praised her school and university achievements but always with a reservation that she had scope to get to a higher level. This has daunted her in all her endeavours, scholarly and artistic.

Religious and political matters do not intrude into her private life. Friends are struck by her a-political and religious stances. Follow your own agendas has been Peta's catch cry. She disregards external dictates and urgings of how to frame an outlook and commitments to life. Her upbringing meant that an independent and self-reliant personal philosophy, initiated by her parents, would carry over into her adult life. And this has been the approach to her children and her relationships with her husband and others.

Every brush stroke Peta makes reminds her that she is in control of what matters most. Art represents her determination to progress while comforted by a positive family life.

Ross

Libraries are one of the temples of civilisation in the view of retired town-planner and avid reader, Ross. Assailed by technological upheaval and funding cuts, they remain one of the stalwarts for transmitting the world of ideas and imagination to the community. Ross sees them as sanctuaries where he can consider and reflect. In his early sixties, the divorcee feels he has to maintain the discipline of self-improvement and devote some time to delve into and explore what his preferred media and literature offer.

Library visits are part of his fortnightly routine. Since retirement the bespectacled Ross has gone to lengths to maintain dress standards when in public. In the library you will find him neatly attired with fashionable shirts, pressed slacks and polished shoes. He is always well -groomed and manicured which together with his pale complexion, lean body and 175cm height suggest a man of means and middle-class upbringing. His full shock of greying hair suggests a person of experience and wisdom. Without spectacles, friends claim he is the spitting image of George Clooney, which he rejects, but not too earnestly.

When not using the internet or nose down in his favourite journal, The Economist, Ross allows his eyes to drift from the screen or page to take in the library and its occupants. Recent relaxation of behaviour rules for library users has annoyed him. His pet hate is unruly infants whose parents allow them to meander noisily around the library. Talking patrons also annoy. Attracting his attention, when she is on duty, is a middle-aged casual librarian whom he finds attractive. He has a silent passion for her. Alluring is her tall elegance, her stylish dress sense and tasteful face and body jewellery. Her wonderful bright appearance is always set off with the most exotic long ear rings reminding him of beautiful Tzigane women. He is summoning the courage to befriend and assess whether she is likely to be a candidate for a future date.

Ross has dated sporadically since an amicable divorce eight years ago and following a 29 year childless marriage. Neither had intended to have children. Not one of his dates turned out to be suited for a long-term relationship. He is perplexed and cannot understand why he is apprehensive about befriending this librarian who, from the odd interaction and other signs, appears approachable and congenial.

When tired of reading, Ross muses about the lives of fellow patrons, many of whom he sees regularly. In his mind he dredges up hypotheticals about their habits and viewpoints. He wonders whether they sometimes do the same about him. Several times, when having a time out from reading, he has e-mailed the odd letter to council, making suggestions about library layouts and logistics to improve patron experience. He has never received a response.

A sunny and airy three bedroom apartment, purchased after his divorce, is Ross's pride and joy. He redecorated it and fitted out a bedroom as a library and study. The apartment is meticulously maintained and cleaned. Friends compliment his fastidiousness and his taste in furnishings and wall hangings. They also enjoy his dinner parties and fine cooking. His wardrobe is a model of orderliness, with shoes and clothing stored and hung with military precision. Following a Japanese tradition, visitors remove their shoes on entering and are provided with house slippers. An only child, he has photos of his late parents both in his bedroom and lounge.

Occasionally, Ross will travel to the city to visit its two major art galleries, religiously taking morning coffee at their cafes overlooking the harbour. Being a conservative and traditionalist, he has not been impressed by some of the off-beat installations and contemporary paintings. Drysdale is his favourite artist and he rues the day he never invested in his art when he received money from his parents' estate. Sometimes he will meet up with a cousin for coffee in the Strand Arcade, which is his favourite city building.

A long-time and enthusiastic golfer, Ross joins senior groups once or twice a month to play at local courses and occasionally at outer Sydney courses. Golfing matches his temperament and competitive spirit, although he is disappointed that his low handicap has blown out through lack of practice. He has been a member of a club, but relinquished his membership because the etiquette, the sportsmanship code and social aspects of golfing were eroding and spoilt by new members, who did not value the traditions of the game. Ross could not stand ill-tempered and aggressive behaviour during competitive rounds of golf. As well, the amiable post-match social drinks had evaporated being both a casualty of drink-driver laws and of time-scarce players.

Ross's view is that architectural and urban planning standards are being lowered, as regulators allow a less exacting approach to design, construction and inspection to prevail. Quality and aesthetics are being traded away when political and economic interests drive hasty and tasteless development. While he keeps in contact with former colleagues at work, he is slowly allowing these links to discontinue, as he tires of their endless talk about their former world of work and indulging in mindless nostalgia.

International holidays and travel are a must for Ross. Southern Europe and east coast USA are his favoured destinations, especially major cities. Pedestrian traffic has been a long-term interest and wherever he goes he notes how cities cater for pedestrians. Elevated walkways, pedestrian malls, garden passage ways, divided footpaths, interlinked alley ways, subways, travelators and walkways draw his attention, whenever they solve congestion and access problems. There is no better way for Ross to relax than to enjoy a long lunch in small restaurants, especially in the old quarters of the cities of Spain and Italy. The ever-prepared Ross always travels with spare coat hangers, a wash basin stopper and several bull-dog clips to peg out any hand-washed laundry.

There is no fear of the future for Ross who is confident that there are no obstacles, apart from a health mishap, that will limit his enjoyment of life. For the future a more intellectual stimulation will be sought and he is weighing up the options of doing a Psychology program at university, either on-line or through normal tuition. Behavioural antics of politicians and media stars always fascinate him and he thinks psychological training will provide him a means to understand their behaviour. He is confounded by how some high-profile media people have a seemingly hypnotic hold on audiences.

The world of ideas and travel give Ross much enjoyment as does ordering the affairs of his everyday life. A romantic involvement would be the icing on his cake of life.

Ahmed

Fishing the bays and inlets of the harbour give taxi driver, Ahmed, relief from the long hours behind the wheel and a welcome respite from his cloistered home life with his aging parents. Driving night shifts free him, throughout the working week, to have uncrowded daytime access to favoured wharf, rock and wall fishing spots during the right tidal condition. He never fishes at weekends and takes pride in formulating his own bait which is based on fresh chicken and cooking oil. Aware of fishery conservation, Ahmed returns undersize catches to the harbour. His edible catches are taken home, where his mother will cook a favourite fish dish for his invalid father.

The approach of his 35th birthday reminds Ahmed, an unmarried IT graduate, that life is passing him by. Despite attempts by his parents and others to introduce him to potential wives, he is largely without female company. He fears a married life is eluding him. His main social outlet is weekend dinners with old friends, whom he met on his course at university. He deeply resents that his course and training yielded no permanent appointment in the IT industry. His only IT exposure comes from his taxi colleagues and their children, who need IT assistance from time to time.

Ahmed

Responsible and caring is how Ahmed's family regard him. The mortgage on the unit, where he and parents live, is met by him. His two married sisters live in Beirut and north Queensland and maintain contact. Ferrying his father to the hospital has become a constant call on Ahmed's spare time as has taking his mother shopping. The family has no relatives locally with whom they can socialise. From time to time his cultural obligations to parents are challenging and dominating.

Fishing is all consuming for Ahmed. He does not talk to other anglers and revels in the privacy of fishing and the space it provides for quiet reflection. He has steered away from fishing clubs which do not appeal because of their drinking culture. A long-held desire is to go to North Queensland to fish, but finances and parent responsibility hold him back. When he has no success with fishing, he will sometimes bring home a whole snapper bought at his local seafood shop.

Apart from his taxi uniform, the wiry slightly built, lightly-bearded Ahmed wears conservative clothing. He is conscious of his aquiline features, heavy eyelids and prominent nose. Tracksuits and hooded jackets are favoured for outdoor and casual wear. He is aware of his bandy-leggedness and slight stoop. The only shorts in his wardrobe are ones he used for soccer and which he wore to play with a group of Iraqi friends. A permanent knee injury, three years ago, has ruled out a return to soccer. To keep fit Ahmed exercises every week when he concentrates on his torso for conditioning. Whenever possible, he gets together with his former soccer friends at weekends.

Conversations about his country of birth and its problems are disconcerting. Passengers and neighbours often quiz him about the plight and destiny of his homeland. He will try to divert the onboard chatter by steering conversations to focus on local events and other topics including weather and sport. Proudly Iraqi, he feels disheartened by the long horror his country has endured and conversations only serve to remind him of the destruction his country, with its great history and culture, has suffered. When he visits his local barber shop, run by an Iraqi, he declines to talk about current events in his homeland.

Pride and joy among his possessions is a Mitsubishi Lancer which has been modified for speed and performance. Well maintained and fitted with leather seats, the car occupies the lock up garage in his apartment block. His parents criticise the money and time he spends on the car, including amateur car racing at a local track. For Ahmed, the car is a great diversion, even though it involves more driving. When working on his car, he is removed from the wrangles, tensions and trivia of home and work. An old university friend will often help him tune his car.

Unknown to his parents, Ahmed had a brief romantic relationship with an older woman, whom he met at a car race meeting. They struck up a relationship while watching races and dated for nine months. The intimate relationship gave Ahmed a sense of belonging, as well as confirming the importance of shared sensuality in shaping a sense of self-worth. Without any explanation the woman suddenly broke off the relationship, refusing to meet or to give her reason. A devastated Ahmed searched for possible reasons, knowing that his religion was not an issue between them. His closest friend said that this woman was a male trophy hunter and that Ahmed had to accept that he was a pawn in a conquest game. Despite urgings from his friend, Ahmed will not use on-line dating services.

Taxi driving has afforded an opportunity to hear the views and feelings of locals and visitors. He encounters all races and ethnicities. Sports, politics, weather, music and travel dominate most exchanges. He senses the mood and outlook of many passengers and finds it surprising how much people reveal of their private lives. Early days of taxi driving introduced him to the rich array of language from his Australian fares. Words like 'balltearer', 'bludger', 'arsey', 'derro', 'grundies', 'hoon', 'alcos' and 'drongo' had him puzzled for a time.

Mobile phones have killed a lot of passenger and driver chat which Ahmed misses, particularly when he has large amounts of idle time in his evening shift. And he wonders whether he is an exception, rarely experiencing racism or abuse from passengers. Other drivers marvel at Ahmed's ability to generate fares. Knowledge of location, time and evening peculiarities enable Ahmed to optimise his fare collection, frequently achieving 20 percent more than others working the same shift.

Driving and fishing provide ample time for Ahmed to review his life and prospect. He is envious of those in his friendship circle who are married with children, have fulfilling jobs and an extended family. In some ways he feels trapped, unable to shift his life away from his present situation. As the only son he feels an obligation to care for his parents and is mildly resentful that his sister, who runs a large logistics business, never invites her parents for a holiday on her large estate in Queensland. Although even tempered, Ahmed gets frustrated with his mother's complaints and observations about his personal habits. On occasions he vents his displeasure, buts keep it subdued out of respect for his parents. Overriding all his concerns is the quest to find a wife to build a new life, where children and companionship will transform his life.

Ahmed feels that there is an urgency to change direction and to experience the special love of a wife and children. He struggles with parental obligations and traditional behaviour codes, which shackle him and limit opportunities for a better life.

Don

At least once a week bachelor Don washes and vacuums his Hyundai Genesis and, if necessary, blackens its tyres. Housed in a large garage attached to his late parents' house the Hyundai is surrounded by tools and car paraphernalia, accumulated by his late mechanic father. The garage housed Australian Fords and Holdens before Don introduced the Korean interloper to the ordered and dust free vehicle stable. The low mileage, pristine Hyundai receives endless pampering.

A former army catering corps officer, Don works four evenings a week as a venue manager for a large hospitality company. Life in the army, and now, in the private sector, have given the athletic 47 year old a range of leadership and organisational skills. These blend well with his style of working, where he sets schedules and targets as the means of personally monitoring his performance. Don feels that his 185cm height adds to his presence and authority when managing operations. His exit interviews in the army affirmed that Don was a classic finisher, never leaving loose ends and always ensuring all projects were completed in accordance with guidelines.

Don attributes his obsession with the car to his father, who instilled regular habits of car care and maintenance.

Don knows he is the butt of jokes from friends about the tending to his Genesis. Friends are amazed about the amount of cleaning and polish materials that are kept in the garage and the car boot. After driving, Don checks his car before garaging, taking care to remove bird droppings, tar spots and insect splatters. He never parks near or under Moreton Bay fig trees. When hosing down his car in the driveway, Don takes great caution to ensure that suds are dispersed over the front lawn. Passengers are never allowed to eat or drink in the car.

A small circle of friends enjoys Don's company. He is the consummate host, entertaining regularly at home with wine and cheese tastings, lunchtime barbecues and occasional dinner parties. Sometimes the latter are co-hosted with a girlfriend. Don is an active member of a bushwalking club, where he has a network of lady friends happy to share hosting. He has had a no-strings sexual relationship with two of these ladies. Marriage is not a priority for the dapper Don, who loves the company of women. Don's married sisters marvel at this latter-day Don Juan, who is never without the company of women. His mates refer to him as the catering Casanova.

Australia day barbecues are held every year for Don's neighbours and close friends of his late parents. A standard practice at these get togethers is that guests bring a small car-related gift. Among the gifts have been chamois, car deodorant, fabric restorer, dashboard carpet, St Christopher medal, Australian flag sticker and witty bumper stickers which are consigned to a storage cabinet in the garage. All guests wear car-themed shirts or hats, the most popular being treasured Jack Brabham baseball caps. The day concludes with Don proposing a toast to his parents who were loved by all.

Neighbours love Don's readiness to assist and advise on most matters, carrying on the legacy of the good-hearted and generous spirit of his parents. Don has petitioned council on their behalf, paid for the removal of a diseased tree threatening nearby houses, secured the eviction of troublesome tenants of a neighbour, campaigned successfully for road and footpath repaving and lobbied the local MP on traffic issues. One Christmas, he hired a mobile car detailer to refurbish an elderly neighbour's Toyota Corolla. Don has given all his contact details to all his neighbours, and he insists they use these whenever there is a need for support.

Despite his goal driven personality, there is room for fantasy and daydreaming in his quieter moments. At times he allows imagination to take hold. Included among his fantasies are dating a popular TV announcer, whose sharp features and ample bosom entrance him, attending a royal ball with Princess Margaret of Denmark, appearing as a compere at a Tony Bennet concert, sailing the Mediterranean with Cher and winning a Dakar car rally. While Don is happy with his life, his one regret was not to take his Dad to the Monaco Grand Prix - a visit his father always dreamed about. Don always kept a scrapbook for his father of the Grand Prix, its drivers, cars and news reports.

Bushwalking has been his preferred way to exercise and spend his leisure time. The organisational and planning aspects, as well as the challenges of exploring new terrains, strongly appeal to Don. Most of the walks in the upland ranges of NSW have been completed. It is usual to do walks over two to four days with his club. Female walkers of all vintages and capacities enjoy walks when the dashing Don leads. His authority, bonhomie, bushcraft, caring and magnetism explain his popularity. The clarity of his directions and encyclopaedic knowledge of the Australian bush mean that the group leave a walk, feeling that their physical accomplishments are matched by new insights into Australian flora, fauna and geology.

Don's silent fear is cancer, especially prostate, with which his father, uncles and paternal grandfather all had deadly encounters before they reached 70. Not given to hypochondria, he imagines that he also will fall victim, even though tests to date show no evidence. Advice on homeopathic and other natural methods or products for preventing cancer are disregarded. He monitors all articles and websites regularly for new understanding and treatments, realising that there may be no breakthrough in his lifetime. Don regularly donates to cancer research.

Friends jest that his midlife crisis period is approaching, explaining that the psychological dimensions of this will even outwit the all-confident Don. While not taken seriously, he has observed that some men do go off the rails with behaviour following unpredictable pathways. He cannot see how his way of life and habits of thinking will allow this to intrude on his relationships and activities. All this crisis jesting and ribbing from friends have worn thin. Don is resolved that he will emerge unscathed.

Cherishing and upholding his parent's ideals and pursuing a programmed existence have given Don a somewhat dream passage in life. His parents would be proud.

Ivy

~ CLEANING LADY ~

Running a successful home cleaning business for six years gives 51 year old widowed Ivy, a migrant from Hong Kong, considerable satisfaction. With the help of her younger sister and a small crew, she has built a thriving operation throughout the Inner West. Business has grown through references, word of mouth and letter box advertisements. Clients praise her courtesy, industriousness and profession- alism, as well going the extra yard when conditions demand. All job assignments are carefully noted and confirmed by email or text. In most weeks she has a full book of jobs and does weekend jobs where clients have issues with time or commitments.

Ivy's quiet demeanour belies a strong character and a steely business resolve. Clients are amazed at her youthfulness and her attractiveness. Her athletic figure, finely boned face, bright eyes, and shiny black hair complement her positive and cheerful personality. She misses her adult son, who lives abroad but has no lingering grief for her deceased husband, who maintained a cool and remote relationship throughout their 22 year marriage. She looks after her elderly mother in their small cottage at Ashfield.

Never amazed or perplexed by her clients' household conditions, Ivy surmounts all the surprises and challenges.

Piles of dirty laundry, mountains of unwashed dishes, filthy bathrooms and kids' debris do not faze her, but occasionally, the amount of unattended pet 'dirt' does trouble her. Her clients' house conditions range from absolute slovenliness to the clinically pristine. Some clean up before her arrival whilst others leave the house as a virtual pigsty. Her sister is more critical of the way some households do not uphold basic hygiene standards, especially when there are young children at home.

Clients sense that Ivy sees them as a kind of extended family. Whenever people are sick at home, Ivy often assists with errands and other support tasks. She has taken sick clients to the local surgery, when other family members were unavailable. In some ways, long-standing clients have become part of her world, where her understanding and compassion are welcomed by them. Her sister remains detached, preferring to keep involvements impersonal and is quietly critical of Ivy's attachment. There are many moments when Ivy cannot see why her sister wants to work in the business.

Attending to her mother keeps Ivy busy, but she is careful to reserve personal time for leisure, including visits to clubs for meals and catching up with friends. There was a romantic interlude some time back, when she met a widowed Chinese gentleman from Malaysia. They had 18 months in a relationship, spending time dining and occasional weekends interstate. His business commitments were heavy and the relationship ceased when he returned home to Malaysia to take care of business interests. Ivy treasured this time reminding her of the uplift and pleasure experienced when you are able to share deep intimacy with another person.

Her sister cannot understand Ivy's devotion to her mother who, in her view is a selfish, cranky, irritable old lady, plagued by obsessive hypochondria, with unexplained and hardened resentment on all manner of things. She had a falling out with their mother, who told Ivy that her sister's behaviour and lifestyle did not respect her culture and family. Ivy knows that reconciliation is a forlorn hope. Ivy's patience and forbearance does not seem to be affected by their mother's behaviour. There have been unsuccessful attempts to introduce the mother to seniors' social events for retired Chinese, but these have failed.

Realising she is at an important stage in her life, Ivy ponders options for the years ahead. She feels her choices are not handicapped by a shortened period of high schooling. One option includes expanding the business, but she sees the downsides to this, especially in controlling work standards when using extra casual labour. Her other thought is to sell up and develop an import business, focussing on cleaning products and equipment. A relative has a warehouse which she could rent on reasonable terms. He has contacts with suppliers in China as well as contacts with local cleaning firms. One thing she is certain of is that retirement is not part of her thinking.

Ivy always delights in visits to China and the major centres of Shanghai and Hong Kong. Their vibrancy and cultural dimensions elevate and stimulate. There she drives an agenda of indulgence. Walking the old quarters of the cities never disappoints, nor does joining relatives for a meal or shopping trip. Opportunities to add to her wardrobe are not neglected when she explores her favourite fashion outlets. Her sister, envious of Ivy's figure, cannot but admire her clothing choices, which add to her subdued beauty.

Clients and others feel there is a mysterious quality about Ivy's character. Her public persona suggests a determined, balanced, warm, and confident lady at ease with the world.

She contrasts with other local Asian cleaners who do not have Ivy's personality and congeniality. But there is another Ivy, who is desperate to experience a more extraordinary life.

Her hope is to find to an enduring romantic partnership which delivers lots of international travel, fine dining and immersion in the nightlife offered in the cities of Paris and New York. She wants to escape. A somewhat sheltered upbringing, family responsibilities plus the commitment to her cleaning business have so far stymied that aspiration. Her caring and business obligations severely limit the chances of finding someone able to join her in this journey. She longs for gain more social exposure to increase the probability of this ambition. What unnerves her is that this could be a pipe-dream.

Ivy agonizes about the direction she could take, but understands her business and family involvements are difficult to set aside. Romance and travel are important to achieve a balance between the commitments to others and the commitment to self.

Seojun

Born in Australia and raised in Sydney, Seojun, the only son of Korean migrants, balances his life between the demands and pressures of school, family and teenage hood. The conscientious, bespectacled and stringy 14 year old student tries to manage his world of crossed messages and conflicting demands. Jousting with the social imperatives flowing from an adolescent life, a challenging potpourri of culture and traditional family values, all bring stress and never-ending questioning about the future pathways to follow. Compounding his problems are the relentless prompts and images flowing from the E-world.

Generally compliant with school rules, his token rebellion is to leave his school shirt untucked when outside school grounds. He observes the attire, mannerisms and language of contemporaries and, despite censoring from parents, mimics them when he is in adolescent company. When travelling to school on the bus, he likes to keep to himself and focus on his mobile device. He always yields his seat to the elderly whenever conditions are crowded.

His family run a laundry business with their residence on the upper floor where he, his parents and mother's sister are crammed into three small bedrooms. His father is often away playing golf and visiting friends. He feels the pressure from his parents to do well at school, which means there is little demand on him to assist in the business. He resents that he has to attend coaching classes after school. In his view they are laborious and dull. Dentistry is what his parents hope will be his career, but he silently wants to enter the arts profession when he leaves school. His pastime at home is sketching and drawing. He has not returned to play soccer which he did at junior level and remains his favourite sport. The school offers soccer for sport but because it is badly organised and coached, he has discontinued playing there.

Following the urgings of an uncle, he is taking tennis lessons, which he finds challenging and demanding. He has developed a close friendship with another Korean boy at tennis. They have similar interests and both are irked by overbearing parents. On occasions they meet at a fast food restaurant where they discuss their internet findings about how teenagers in Korea are kicking back and becoming resistant to cultural and family traditions. His friend has been a welcoming sounding board, where he discusses his dreams to become involved in drawing and artistic design. They admire the efforts and dedication of his friend's younger sister, who recently became junior golf champion at a local golf course. Both hope that one day Koreans will win Wimbledon and the British open golf championship.

The squabbling of his parents unnerves him. He retreats to his bedroom and tries to block out the bickering. He suspects a lot of this has to do with money, the condition of their business and the time his father is absent from home. There is an issue about unpaid loans, which Seojun knows nothing about. His mother's sister, who keeps neutral on family disputes, often cooks for the family and assists with household chores.

As a Korean Australian, Seojun takes little interest in the tensions, debates and current issues which flow from those events in China, Japan and North Korea affecting Korea's future. Without any special knowledge, Seojun does not get engaged in these historical problems and expresses little interest in current developments on the Korean peninsula. His parents are disappointed by his indifference to Korean economic and political matters. He remains untouched by his parent's antipathy towards China and Japan. He is more interested in the fortunes of Korea in world soccer and other sports.

Secondary schooling is not bringing much joy to Seojun. At primary school he performed well but at high school he flounders in some subjects and is saved by coaching in others. He considers that some of his teachers are lazy. Some cannot teach and others, while enthusiastic and well-meaning, lack organisation and direction. More broadly, he finds that his school is not well managed. Disruptions and discontinuities in and outside the classroom on some days suggest things are in a state of turmoil. His year nine Science class is particularly bad where, with the high turnover of teachers and their poor replacements, perpetual bedlam often reigns. Seojun is quietly contemptuous of some of his fellow students who are openly disrespectful and rude to teachers.

He compares his teachers with his tennis coach. Highly respected, disciplined in a congenial way, confident and an effective instructor, the coach contrasts sharply with the ineffectual corps of teachers he is experiencing. His parents remain unaware of the conditions of his school and the shortcomings of his teachers.

Seojun remains disappointed about his parents' unfulfilled promises to him. He hoped that his parents would have taken him on a vacation to the Gold Coast. This was promised when he finished primary school, but did not eventuate because his mother was ill. There is still no indication that the promise will be fulfilled. A promise to visit Disneyland for his eighth birthday also failed because of major issues with the family business, which he never understood. His mother is vowing she will make good the promises in the not too distant future.

Cascading through his mind sometimes are TV news reports dealing with migration, which sometimes he focuses on whenever the issue of Asian immigrants comes to the fore. While never directly encountering offensive comment on his Korean heritage, he is aware that friends have sometimes received unwelcome remarks in public places. He experiences the odd friendly ribbing about his eyes and hair at sport or school but never encounters any maliciousness. His parents educated him well on how to react if he received abuse. His tactic is to not to shy away but remain positive. As a young teenager he is sensing that there may be times he needs to be more assertive and display pride of his heritage. He thinks, because his school is co-educational and is a cultural 'bouillabaisse', he is not experiencing negative comments about his ethnicity.

Moving into adulthood will pose Seojun challenges, particularly where his preference for future work is at odds with that of his parents. A Korean ancestry is a minor matter when transiting an adolescent world.

Brad and Bernie

~ LOVING PARTNERS ~

Breakfast diners and partners for three years, Brad and Bernie, eagerly look forward to their brunch on Sundays at their favourite local café. A plus, if the weather is right, is to have a footpath table where they scan the Sunday parade of locals and greet friends. They notice that there has been a surge in the growth of leashed dogs joining the parade. Every post and building corner, as well as the pathway, are permanently stained with dog urine. The piddled pavement sours the ambience. They avoid sitting near diners accompanied by their dogs.

On Sundays both are decked out in colourful shirts, tailored jeans, caps and boat shoes. Red-haired, thin-lipped, freckled Bernie, whose angular height is 182cms, towers over Brad. Most times Bernie is conservatively dressed and Sunday is his day for clothing adventure. Brad, who is conscious of his weak chin, slight baldness and watery protruding eyes, wears ear studs, wrist bangles, and is open to contemporary trends in clothing styles and body jewellery. Close friends see Bernie as a lean bean and Brad a plump plum. Brad manages a franchised fashion accessory shop in a nearby shopping mall. Bernie is the manager for a city theatre and deliberately wears sober clothing to distinguish himself from his theatre associates.

BRAD and BERNIE

Both are in their early thirties and came from Queensland, where both have parents living. Brad's parents are unaware of this relationship.

Their nearby apartment overlooks a park where they occasionally picnic with friends. Unlike Brad, Bernie is very house proud, does most of the cooking and adds bits of décor to turn their 60s apartment into a fashionable pad. Brad's untidiness sometimes gets on Bernie's wick, especially when clothes are left about and cups and glasses are unreturned to the dishwasher. Brad's bathroom habits annoy-unflushed toilet, unscoured wash basin, undisposed tissues, uncapped medicine containers and toothpaste tubes. However, Bernie is the ultimate forgiver. Annoyance is quickly dissolved under the charm assault of Brad.

They met at a mutual friend's party and their relationship quickly bloomed. Their wicked sense of humour and shared hostility to most things in Queensland gave them a common ground. The partnership was Brad's first and Bernie's second. Neither are proselytizers of their approach to love; neither are publicly active in advancing the causes of equality and non-discrimination. Same sex marriage is discussed amongst their friendship circle, but it is not a matter of concern for them. Their rent and house costs are equally shared.

They enjoy leisure time together. Both are cricket lovers, enjoying also in recent times basketball. Their big adventure was a trip to Thailand which has become their iconic destination. It was great for their budget and appealed to their aesthetic senses. Low cost accommodation, cheap food, attractive people, rich culture and exotic countryside bowled them over. Bernie's ever-present bronchial condition inhibited some of their gallivanting and boundary breaking during a three week stay. Bernie's attachment to Brad deepened through the loving care and attention given by Brad when Bernie was having a bronchial episode. Bernie bought Brad an expensive gold friendship ring before they left Thailand.

Discussions about the future recur whenever Bernie's work commitments disrupt their social arrangements. Late night finishes, unscheduled meetings and theatre logistics mean that Bernie is sometimes unexpectedly held up or delayed. Many a time Brad has fumed at the irregular hours involved. He accepts that Bernie is dedicated to his work and knows that this is part of the deal when working in the theatre. Brad feels that a looming issue between them is Bernie's desire to work in London, which is of no interest to him whatsoever. Particularly galling is Bernie's continued reference to working abroad when they are with company. He is not game to state openly that going to London will never be on his agenda.

Getting out and about is their mantra when chatting to neighbours. When not working, they like to experience inner Sydney. Pubs, restaurants, stores, cinemas, wine bars, book sellers, markets, galleries and theatres enjoy their patronage. They enthuse about areas like Newtown, avoiding venues with heavy gay patronage. Saving money is not on their agenda. Both are devotees of Thai and Indian food. Brad is occasionally put off by Bernie's approach to eating. He is a very slow eater, lingering over his meal, savouring every mouthful, and in Brad's mind, excruciatingly slow. When approaching his dish, Bernie is like a surgeon dissecting and inspecting every piece of food before spooning or forking in the smallest of portions. Waiters hover wanting to clear Brad's dish, whilst Bernie executes his prolonged mastication and food surgery.

Religion remains important to Bernie. He was raised in a devout Catholic family. The theatre of the church, the mystical aspects of believing and the role of prayer continue to be important. Bernie told his family about his sexual orientation soon after leaving high school and while he was studying dramatic arts. To his surprise, neither parents nor siblings reacted negatively, supporting his situation and encouraging him to pursue his heart, wherever that leads. Outside his immediate social circle, Brisbane's phobias proved too confining forcing him to move to Sydney where he pursued his theatrical interests. Visiting family remains important for Bernie. Parents' birthdays are celebrated with personal visits.

Aimlessness best describes a younger Brad, who had an unstable family life and schooling. Working in retail sales and display enabled Brad to explore his interests in fashion and design. Unsatisfactory and unrewarding jobs drove Brad to change employment before seeking his fortunes in Sydney's retail scene. Rarely did he hold a job for more than a year. Joining a retail franchise chain proved to be an anchoring point, leading to a management position responsible for layouts and merchandising. Unsure of his sexuality, he flitted between male and female relationships, which unsettled Brad, who sought strong, enduring, emotional ties. Meeting Bernie gave him emotional assurance and confidence of self. He rarely contacts his family, who have not been informed of the nature of his relationship with Bernie.

Seemingly undisturbed by surrounding economic, political, social turmoil, they lead a cocooned, hedonistic life. They found romance. They both limit social media exchanges and have minimal interest in media chatter. Immediate issues with work and home dominate conversations together with the world of cricket in summer.

Conscious of keeping vibrancy in their relationship, they are aware that they have an important task to build trust and to maintain their intimacy momentum. They are ever conscious of the fragile and perverse aspects of intimate companionships.

Bernie is buoyed by his relationship, which fits with his aspirations to build a homelife. Brad found stability and security, both in work and love.

Cliff

Travelling twice a week to his volunteer work at the Botanic Gardens gives retired office manager Cliff a pleasant break from retirement routines at home. He finished working six years ago and now the 68 year old has taken on volunteer work, which provides a stress free environment as well as the friendly company of other retirees contributing to the operations of the gardens. On his bus journey to the gardens, Cliff enjoys doing the cryptic crossword from his daily paper. For the journey the crossword has been cut out of the paper and his small satchel is used as backing. The rest of the paper is left with his wife.

Cryptic crosswords have been enjoyed by Cliff for over 15 years and are part of his daily routine. He finds time whether at work, home or on holidays to work a crossword. Before his paper offered a crossword help line, some of his cryptic colleagues would phone to get assistance. New crossword compilers are welcomed by Cliff. The challenge of deciphering their codes provides mental stimulation and a sense of intellectual achievement. Crosswords sourced from British papers challenge him the most, mainly because of their localised clues and references. He sees on-line crosswords extending his enjoyment.

A happy marriage and supportive home life are cherished by Cliff who believes he is blessed to have a loving wife, three children and four grandchildren. One unmarried son, handicapped through a serious car accident five years ago, lives at home. Cliff introduced him to crosswords with which he has only shown a mild interest. Never daunted Cliff tries to encourage him whenever he senses his son's mood is cheery and positive. Cliff's wife has no interest, preferring TV shows and gardening as leisure pursuits. They both enjoy ABC radio during the day favouring morning sessions and their interviews.

'Cryptics' were a solace for Cliff whenever he encountered tensions or disputes in his management job. He would use tea and lunch breaks to bury himself in a crossword either in his office or the canteen. At his retirement party he was given a T shirt, barbecue apron and underwear all with crossword grid imprints. At the party he learnt that his office nickname was 'one across' which he found hilarious. Farewell gifts included a giant pencil emblazoned with Cliff's name and a plastic box full of erasers.

Years of sedentary work, little exercise, and irregular gardening activity has meant he is not as fit as his doctor would like. His 83kgs weight is a concern. His small thick-set stature carries a slight paunch. Recently he has developed a stoop which is accentuated by not walking upright and holding his head up to reveal a friendly, ruddy face. At the botanic gardens he finds he has to rest frequently and prefers tasks where he can sit. When outside in the sun, Cliff wears conventionally-brimmed headwear regarding the wearing of baseball caps as vulgar and useless. He refused to wear the company logoed caps issued at his work Christmas parties. And he loathes seeing his grandchildren wearing them demanding they remove them when entering his house.

His pet hate is seeing caps worn by diners in restaurants and cafes.

Maintaining an optimistic outlook on most matters has characterised Cliff's life. His wife marvels that he is rarely downcast. News of wars, sordid affairs, criminal behaviour and political scandals do not interest Cliff. He prefers good news stories. Brought up by a religious family has been an asset for Cliff who takes a charitable view when faced with controversy and conflict. He feels his upbringing gave a handy moral compass to guide his decisions and his inter-actions with family and others. At times he found himself a willing listener and sometime counsellor to colleagues who were facing personal difficulties. Offering to assist the needy has passed through Cliff's mind and he plans to do charity work when he gives up his involvement with the botanical gardens.

A conservative taste in clothing has been his daughter's observation about Cliff's wardrobe, both when he was working and now in retirement. He did move to non-iron shirts once they became part of the apparel landscape at work. His suits and ties reflected his conservative tastes and he never wore braces. Current dress trends of executives are criticised by Cliff who regards the current fashion of open-necked shirts with suits and casual shoes as undignified. Old fashioned two-piece flannelette pyjamas continue to be his nightwear, preferring cord tie-ups to elastic waist bands. He refuses to wear a colourful nightshirt bought for his 60th birthday.

A long concern of his wife has been his physical health and diet. His diet breaks many guidelines for a healthy heart and waistline. Among his food vices are two sugars with tea and coffee, full cream milk, biscuits or cake with morning and afternoon tea, ice cream with desserts, lots of butter and salty foods. Alcohol is occasionally drunk at special celebrations. Cliff has been troubled with a hernia for which he continues to defer medical attention. Recently he has been suffering reflux and ignores his wife's advice to go to the doctor and get it treated properly. His wife urges him, with no success, to attend physical exercise classes for seniors, held at a local church hall.

A continuing concern for Cliff is whether his retirement savings and pension will be adequate for him and his wife. Money which he had left from an estate had been placed in low risk investments. On advice from a friend, a financial adviser, he shifted some of this money into higher earning assets offered by a high-profile investment firm. The money was lost in some unexpected corporate collapses. He rues the day he abandoned his conservative position to seek potentially higher returns. He counts his blessings that he is mortgage free and there is always money to take a vacation. He remains on good terms with his adviser friend, regarding the advice was well-intentioned.

Trends in broadcasting unsettle Cliff who finds many TV comedy shows and documentaries falling short of entertainment standards he enjoyed in the past. There is over use of expletives and the attempts at comedy and satire are pathetic. Documentaries appear to be uninformative and err towards the bad rather than the good in the world. Both he and his wife agree there is too much emphasis on the negatives rather than the positives of Australia. They always enjoy knowledge-quiz programs.

Cliff enters his twilight years feeling he has responded well to the messages advising how to enjoy retirement. Armed with his crosswords, a loving family and volunteer work he believes he is placed well to enjoy life's bounties.

Dylan

~ CARING DAD ~

Early evenings see Dylan carrying his baby son Jack for an outside walk to settle him down. Jack is front-harnessed and peers forward as Dylan strides along the footpaths in the fading light. Dylan embraces fatherhood, taking all opportunities to share time with Jack. The bearded, gaunt, bespectacled and lanky 32 year old council administration officer sings softly to Jack as they move around their suburb. Jack is always bedecked in a colourful beanie which features the colours of Dylan's favourite AFL team. Normally they arrive back home in time to greet partner and mother, 34 year old Amy, who owns a child psychology practice in a nearby suburb.

Sleep is not Jack's preferred leisure activity. He refuses all attempts to get him to sleep. Amy's expertise, and both the child carer's and Dylan's ministrations do not yield slumber dividends. When matters become desperate late at night, Dylan will be found strolling the streets with a non-succumbing Jack. Amy, a busy professional with a low patience threshold, retreats to bed leaving Dylan to manage Jack's slumber arrangements. Feeding Jack and carrying out toilet routines are left largely to Dylan and the daytime child carer.

The relationship between Dylan and Amy is now in its in seventh year. Jack was planned ostensibly to satisfy their deep desire to be parents. Soon after Jack's arrival both agreed that Dylan would be the lead parent because his local council job was low pressure, with flexible hours and attractive parenting allowances. Their recently renovated cottage is fitted with an electronically monitored nursery, together with modern baby ware and appliances. Jack takes pride and place in the photo galleries in the hallway, main bedroom and lounge. Friends note that formula-fed Jack is rarely seen in the arms of Amy.

Jack's photos, relentlessly updated, appear on all family social media sites. Dylan's parents at Ballina are enchanted with their only grandchild, whose image is at saturation level in their albums and sideboard picture frames. Dylan's sister's baby shower present, an over - sprung baby carriage, is rejected by Jack preferring a harnessed Dylan as his transport. Jack does not tire Dylan, who exhibits a dedication and patience, which astounds his cycling mates, who marvel at his capacity to outstay the severest crying onslaught.

Home duties fall on a weekly cleaner, a baby laundry service, the day carer and Amy's widowed mother, who visits regularly and prepares many evening meals. Dylan also does some home duties and devotes many Sundays, following his weekly cycle group outing, attending to unfinished housework. Amy, consumed with practice issues and catch-up, gives fleeting attention to household matters. Ensuring his wife's career does well and is not diverted by home affairs are Dylan's silent commitment to his partner.

He manages to cope with Amy's voracious sexual appetite which is uncurbed and consistent even through her pregnancy. Dylan met Amy through a mutual acquaintance. Amy had been in a long relationship before meeting Dylan who had infrequent female encounters. They had an intense whirlwind romance before agreeing to live together, buying a property and having Jack. Dylan remains besotted with Amy's ample and dumpy physique. Especially stirring for Dylan is Amy's provocative and arousing nightwear bought from an on-line lingerie retailer.

Friends of Dylan are amazed at his devotion to child caring and dedication to housekeeping. Colleagues at work note he optimises his allowances for parenting and uses his flexible hours judiciously. His stories about Jack at morning tea test the patience of his fellow workers. Colleagues jest that Dylan consider expanding his family so his parenting skills are better exploited. He considers this as a compliment, even though he is aware they are jesting.

Cycling delivers an opportunity to gather with friends and obtain some worthwhile exercise for his sinewy body. Most Sundays his cycling group do early morning long rides followed by a chat and coffee. Dylan has his bike outfit and helmet in the colours of his AFL team. When old enough he intends to take Jack on bike rides and already has some ideas for likely outings. His cycling group regard him as an excellent cyclist and in his own quiet way he accepts their accolades as well as the nick name they have given him, 'Cadell O'Dylan'.

Amy does not involve Dylan in her business affairs and tries not to raise business matters when at home. They agreed to keep their banking separate, leaving Dylan to meet all household spending. More children are planned once the business is established and is paying its way. Amy is often reminding Dylan that having more children is only likely once she is comfortable with her business.

The issue on which they are divided is diet. Amy despises the vegetarian regime which Dylan maintains. Dylan silently accepts her view and her pursuit of a high protein meat meals. Neither have discussed what will be the diet for

Jack, once he is able to move fully to solids. Dylan's father, a meat eater, always reminds of the importance of protein for Jack and sends emails on articles dealing with healthy diets for young children and the hazards of a vegetarian diet.

Puzzling to Dylan is Amy's lack of conversation and guidance on child rearing. Her professional knowledge and skills are strangely absent when they discuss Jack's development and behaviour. It is as if she lacks confidence in giving advice and is apprehensive in managing Jack. Dylan feels that she is nervous and worries that her suggestions will backfire. This is forever troubling. To date he has not raised this with Amy, fearful that she may not react well to his observations. He searches for explanations for her reluctance and hesitancy to offer advice about Jack.

The walks with Jack, although trying on occasions, give Dylan opportunities to immerse in the delights of bonding and connecting. He trusts, in time, Amy will also bond.

Bob

Retired auto electrician, Bob, is always working around his cottage to keep it and the surrounds in pristine condition. While his wife mocks his commitments to order, neatness and cleanliness, Bob remains undeterred, believing it is a mark of good citizenship to uphold standards. His home draws comments from locals, who marvel at the attention to maintenance, layout and the pursuit of perfection. Keeping his cottage impeccable energises Bob, who does not need diet or exercises to look after his small nuggety body. He has maintained a weight around 65 kilograms for most of his adult life. His two married sons share Bob's build.

Carried over from his days of running a small auto business, Bob adheres to a regular, daily schedule to check out the surrounds of his property, particularly the front and back yards. The layouts of lawns and gardens are clinically precise, following a formal horticultural template of flowers, shrubs, vegetables and screening plants. This has been extended to his verge where an ordered arrangement of small trees and flowers flourish and are scrupulously tended. All fences are well maintained including attached lattices in the rear garden. He quickly adopted steel edging for garden beds. Not a weed can be found in the soft-buffalo grass lawns, including the grassed section of the verge.

Bob regularly patrols his front footpath, street gutter, fence line and driveway, removing litter, leaves, animal droppings and debris.

Waste collection bins have challenged Bob's sense of order. Bin nights, normally a Monday, and the mornings of collection see Bob galvanised into action. He puts out the scheduled coloured bins, ensuring they are carefully aligned with the footpath edge. He will also align adjacent neighbours' bins if not properly placed. After collection the following morning, Bob retrieves bins which are scattered along his street. He returns immediate neighbours' bins as well. He inspects his bins before washing them out by applying a disinfecting bin cleaner which he has prepared from cheap liquid cleaners. He argues with his wife about her carelessness in placing waste in the wrong bins, which means on some collection evenings he is seen transferring waste to its proper bin. This encourages much derision from his wife.

Bob seethes whenever he finds bags of dog poo deposited in his bins after collection. He is thinking of rising early on collection mornings and catching the poo dumpers red-handed. He is forced to upturn the bins and remove the bags which are then taken to a local park bin designed for dog droppings. Unknown to Bob, his neighbours have a standing joke about Bob's bin management routines. Unkindly, a neighbour refers to St. Bob as the patron saint of bins.

A former employee, Morris, visits Bob regularly. Together in his work shed they spend hours making wooden letter boxes, which Morris sells at weekend community markets. Bob designed some unique patterns based on bird designs for the letter box flaps. Through befriending a local timberyard, Bob gets off-cuts of wood at near zero cost for the boxes. Morris understands Bob clinical nature and is happy to work in a secondary role, leaving the materials and assembly work to follow Bob's patterns. He accepts criticism whenever his workmanship is not up to Bob's standard.

Morris prefers Bob not to work at the markets. He can create difficulties by interfering with sales pitches and display arrangements. Privately Morris considers him a pain in the arse on market days. If he attends, Bob is constantly moving around critically commenting to him on other vendors' pitches. A vendor once took Bob to task for commenting on the encroachment of his stall into common space. The aggrieved vendor told Bob to bugger off and stop being an old woman. Morris's intercession calmed matters.

A continuing disappointment for Bob is the apparent the lack of appreciation from his neighbours for his efforts to keep their locality tidy and to improve communal responsibilities. His proposal to set up a neighbourhood watch failed, because he tried to set a watch regime which his neighbours found laughable. They also tire of Bob's continual railing against the standard of council services and the sloppiness of their employees. While listening to Bob's rants, they try to divert conversation to a different topic. They have sympathy for Bob's wife but accept, at heart, Bob is a generous and a well-meaning person.

As much as she can, his wife discourages him from accompanying her on her weekly grocery shop. He has been known to question supermarket employees on their shelf layouts, pointing out that the placement of heavy products on bottom shelves creates unnecessary strain on elderly shoppers. His critical commentary on how shopping bags are packed simply infuriates, forcing her to bite her tongue. She wishes she had the fortitude to kick him in the shins when he starts up commentary on packing strategies.

Many have wondered why Bob has this fastidious streak, which is not shared by his parents or his siblings. Apart from the discipline of running his own business, no one has been able to explain Bob's behaviour. One theory is that he acquired this from his schooling, where he was a compliant pupil and relished the ordered life of school, and from the meticulous training he received as an apprentice. His first employer ran a strict work regime. The young apprentice Bob was responsible for closing the workshop each day. He had to tidy up, clean and return equipment to its correct location, lock away cars, spruce up the lunch room, sweep the office and workshop. At technical college his tutors marvelled at his attentive workmanship and the care exercised when doing practice tasks.

Morris continues to be puzzled by Bob's character. For all his ordered and scheduled life there remains a mystery about the inner Bob. Nothing of a deep personal level is revealed. He is a closed book. How Bob feels about sensual, religious, political and family matters is never disclosed, despite much prompting. It is as if Bob runs on automatic. He only shows emotion when his ordered life gets disrupted. In some ways he is a cold fish. Morris would love to know what Bob's wife thinks.

Bob engages with life sustained by ritual and a self-imposed set of obligations. Satisfaction is achieved through completion of tasks. He assumes others accept his daily way of negotiating life.

David and Di

~ ADORABLE DUO ~

As they enter their 43rd and 41st year respectively, David and Di, partners for six years, consider themselves fortunate to have a wonderful relationship and the prospect of better years ahead. Both are in secure jobs - David an architectural draftsman and Di, a finance broker. They bask in the status of relatively newcomers to Australia; David from England and Di from New Zealand. After getting together, they moved around Sydney, before buying an apartment where they have lived for the past four years. They have no intention of marrying nor of having children. Friends often refer to them as the decorous 'Ds'.

Both are tall and athletic. David has a strong torso and is broad shouldered, while Di has a boyishly slim figure and matches David's height of 181 cms. The startling physical feature of both is that they have long slender hands and long, finely boned feet. Regular exercise and competitive weekend tennis matches keep them both healthy and fit. He has sandy hair whilst she is an ash blonde. They maintain an open diet regime and enjoy all cuisines. Their preference for food is Mediterranean style, with fish being their main source of protein.

When out together they make a handsome couple. Their dress is noted for taste, style and colour matching. David is devotee of R M Williams boots (he has six pairs) while Di wears longish skirts which are flouncy and highly colourful. Where appropriate, she wears high collared blouses and body jewellery with strong Maori motif elements. They shop together for furnishings, clothes and food. Neither is a great saver. The constraint on their spending is the joint servicing of their mortgage. They have a car for weekend visits.

Of the two, David is quieter, less extroverted, more intense, and is an economical conversationalist. He is happy to step back, letting Di take prominence in social gatherings, deferring to her engaging, lively presence, normally accompanied by a wicked Kiwi sense of humour. Mindful of her social prowess, Di is always corralling a compliant David into conversations, as well as placing him strategically at dinner party tables. Slightly concerning for David is that Di occasionally over indulges in alcohol, which can make her irritable the next day. But this is not an issue that David raises with her.

They met following previous relationships that had failed. David rarely mentions this part of his past whilst Di is open about the horrific time she had with her former partner, who was both abusive and financially reckless. Di occasionally recalls these unhappy times whenever she and David have had a special romantic encounter, where Di affirms her good fortune to be with David and being forever blessed that they found each other. Di publicly shows her happiness to be with David by walking arm in arm on their strolls and planting a kiss on his cheek when there is an appropriate moment. On many evenings they walk to a local bay to take in the harbour activity and the evening sky.

The sanctuary of care and love provided by David is highly welcomed by Di. It provides respite from the hectic networked life she encounters in her brokerage. The constant negotiating, dealing and resolving call on her extensive experience and highly tuned interpersonal skills. Her Kiwi directness, together with clarity of communicating, assures a successful life in brokering. Di deploys her social skills with great effect. Mentioning lingering work problems, when at home, is avoided.

Both try to moderate their English and Kiwi accents. Australia is their permanent home and they do not wallow in home country nostalgia. Both now have Australian passports. David is aware that his accent does grate with some colleagues, who remind him light-heartedly of his British derivation. He is an avid supporter of Australian sporting teams as well as a social member of a rugby club. Di retains a pride in her country of origin but realises that, socially and professionally, the de-emphasis of Kiwi vestiges gives more local leverage and acceptance. However, she does use her international Kiwi business networks to advance her brokerage business.

The pulse of their homelife is governed by Di's professional commitments. She is an early riser, leaving for work around 6.30 am and returning normally by 7pm. This suits David, whose office runs a flexible regime of work, permitting him to undertake some work assignments from his office at home. Weekends are devoted to housekeeping, tennis, theatre or movies and dining with friends. They uphold a tacit agreement on sharing home duties. Di struggles to hold to this but David happily and calmly takes on her share where necessary. Friends remind Di that she has won the lottery with David, claiming that apart from being handsome and gentlemanly, David possesses those fine qualities of thoughtfulness, compassion and trustworthiness.

Outwardly Di is confident, fireproof and positive. Before meeting David, she would have entered some dark spaces, resulting from the abuse from her previous partner. She lacked assuredness and a sense of worth. To cope, she undertook therapy and counselling as well as resorting to anti-depressants. She met David soon after recovering from her treatment. An old girlfriend, who witnessed her recovery, attributed the turn around to the support and caring received from David.

Both plan for another ten years of work, after which they contemplate a complete change of pace and location. They occasionally spend weekends in the Mudgee region of NSW which appeals. They intend buying a small rural retreat there, to build a cottage, to grow their own produce, and to run a small consultancy on lifestyle change, involving a rural housing and financing advisory service for those seeking a rural life.

David reflects on his good fortune to have met someone to share his future. He is prone, when in a daydreaming phase, to pause over his work and think about what it means to have a loving companionship. At one level, to have close intimacy and emotional reciprocity is clearly a plus, whilst at another level the practical and operational aspects of living together as an effective pair is important. He feels elated that he is enjoying a relationship which delivers affection and support.

Looking ahead, they have those partnership elements which underwrite a durable relationship. Apart from death, they feel there is nothing which will upset their journey together.

Rona

Early morning on Iron Cove sees Rona joining other adult rowers, stroking their way around the Cove's rowing course. All are in pursuit of building strength and stamina, as well as toning up their torsos and limbs. Rona is now in her second year of rowing, joining a group of women seeking exercise and diversion. There is a streak of rebellion in Rona, who took up rowing in the face of some mocking, as well as opposition from her husband and two near adult sons, who are now forced to prepare their own breakfasts and lunches and to find their clothes in the unironed laundered pile in the sunroom.

Rowing is a perfect escape from her blokey household, offering new friends, a peaceful outdoors environment, and physical exercise. Early menopause has not deterred the former accounts clerk from tackling the challenges of rowing. Apart from the fitness aspects, rowing has generated positive feelings about her 172cm, slightly built body, which became unfit after she stopped work a year ago when she turned 48. This positive charge has Rona experimenting with long hairstyles, dress outfits and makeup. The transformation has brightened her features – her slouch has gone and her button-nose is overshadowed by sparking eyes and an ever-sunny face.

Rona

The new Rona notes her blokes at home rarely comment on her changes, especially the transfiguring and titivation.

Her fellow rowing companions are a mixed bunch, whose ages range between 42 and 56, and most of whom possess athletic physiques. Some are working whist others, like Rona, are at home with children at high school and college. There is honesty in her group, able to talk openly about improving their rowing performance as well as issues emerging in their last row. Rona is surprised how much mental lift is experienced following a hard row. This allows her to override the mundaneness of home life. She never tires of the routines accompanying the preparation and conclusion of each row. Especially loved are her rowing T-shirts which are emblazoned with a scull motif in pink.

Rona cannot wait for her rowing days. Even when the weather conditions are marginal, she never shies away from her mornings on the water. There is special elation when she rows out on clear, calm days, experiencing the wakening signs of a new day. What surprises her is that the initial muscle and other aches experienced in early days of rowing have largely disappeared. And paradoxically, the rowing has impacted positively on how she goes about scheduling tasks at home. She finds tasks are done quickly and she has more time for herself. The management of her sons has become a dream with her new energy and mental toughness. She calmly deflects or dismisses their complaints and surliness, reminding them they are old enough to manage their own affairs and to take on more responsibility.

There is some unease with her husband, who is not reacting well to Rona's new lease on life. Whilst never a subdued character, Rona now is more assertive and quite prepared to remind her husband, Blaine, of a partner's duties, as well arguing her point of view, whenever he raises marital and household problems. Residual tensions and moping are a thing of the past when Rona takes to the water, allowing all relationship issues to evaporate under the splash of her oars. Her husband now gets a jovial scolding if past matters or disputes are raised. Despite her suggestion, Blaine has no interest in taking up rowing to keep fit.

Rowing constantly reminds her of the problem of pollution, which becomes more obvious in the cove following rain. Plastics, bottles, dead domestic animals and street litter are regularly encountered. Sometimes, when there is a low tide, she joins her cajoled sons on weekends to gather rubbish left beached along a stretch of the nearby foreshore. All now are volunteers on clean-up campaigns.

Sport was never Rona's long suit. At school and in the years before marriage, Rona did not play sport, and exercise was limited to walking the family dog and walking to bus stops. Her embrace of rowing surprised her, as did the psychological and physical rewards it delivered. In her extended family she now has to check herself from repeating the benefits derived from her newly found sport. Her sisters, both of whom are older than Rona, quietly remind her that this championing of rowing is wearing thin and is teetering on becoming somewhat tedious.

To close friends, the enthusiastic and zealous immersion of Rona in rowing is not a surprise. Her personal history is full of causes and commitments which had been pursued unrelentingly, until events like marriage, child bearing or job changes brought them to a halt. Famously, she was known for her campaigns on vegetarianism, until a doctor told her she should boost protein to maintain a healthy pregnancy. Friends remind Blaine that he should be proud of what Rona is achieving.

Middle age is a regular concern for Rona. Both her parents died before 70 through circulation diseases. Rona, through medicals, has no indication of inheriting the same health problems. Her feeling is that rowing has delivered a firewall, assuring a healthy existence well into her senior years. On all the metrics to gauge her health, Rona's doctor has her highly rated. The only concern has been the emergence of spider-web veins on her legs which she considers unsightly. The fact she can wear fetchingly long dresses with her slim shape has been a boon in this regard.

Triggering Rona's business sense is an advice request from a friend, who is a female sports fashion designer. She believes the sports apparel market is ripe for new shapes and colours which are aligned with rowing. She wants Rona's ideas on designs of tops which enhance bare shoulders and arms. Rona is providing feedback, based on her observations of colleagues' physiques and the colours which tune well with water backgrounds. This undertaking reminds Rona of how attractive proportionately strong shoulders add to a woman's look and sexiness.

For Rona, rowing has become a metaphor for living a positive life. Elements for such a life include cooperation, commitment, thorough preparation and execution, a positive mindset and a personal improvement momentum.

Walter

Walter, a retired English teacher, likes to keep physically active by taking long and high-tempo walks three to four days a week. He does not count his steps. Starting usually at 7am he follows the same walking route because it gives him a variety of undulations as well as pleasant scenery of the harbour and its islands. He greets a number of regulars on his path, adding to the enjoyment of his morning constitutional. Thankful that his wife of 34 years does not join him, the tall, willowy 61year old relishes the solitude and quietness, which he finds difficult to arrange since retiring two years ago.

Conscious of his appearance when walking, he is always cleanshaven and well- groomed, which emphasises his well chiselled facial features. The acknowledgement by his doctor that he has praiseworthy health metrics for his age, together with an unblemished medical history, give him quiet pride. Always alert to physiques, he notes the wondrous shapes of his fellow walkers as they approach him. He endeavours to build categories in his mind of the human contours he observes. Of late, Walter has adopted his own 'umpy' scale to slot approaching females into categories: bumpy, dumpy, frumpy, humpy, jumpy, lumpy, 'pumpy', rumpy, 'tummpy' and 'yummpy'. He looks forward, especially when the 'yummpies' approach, these being attractive ladies with shapely bodies. One of the regular mature female walkers greets him as if he was a long-time friend. He muses that she is perhaps unattached and may have designs on him.

He looks forward to returning home, when his wife is away visiting or doing charity work. He then takes long hot showers followed by freshly brewed coffee, which he has with an almond croissant, bought from his local patisserie. Whenever she is at home, he has short showers before having morning tea with her, whilst they read the morning papers before progressing to their crosswords. His wife rarely enquires about his walks and both look forward to weekly skyping their only offspring, a daughter, who is working in a gallery in London. They have a caring relationship where intimacy is proportionate to their mature age.

Walking gives time to reflect about the standards of English in schools and in the media. He detests truncation of the language, arising from texting and emails. The language is being hollowed out and crippled. He detests the lack of care in language use. The confusion of the use of the word 'good', the adjective, and 'well', the adverb, by radio commentators gets him especially riled. His campaigns for correct spelling and punctuation at school were largely ignored by his fellow teachers, who seemed disinterested in forcing students to adhere to standards.

Now, as in the past, Walter eases his anguish about English usage by wrapping himself in the comforting shawls of great literature and drama. He still marvels at the craft of Oscar Wilde and modern writers like McEwan and Coetzee. His friends get sick of his idolising of Barry Humphries, whom he regards as the best exponent of the Australian vernacular, especially in delivering imagery and comedy. He has a deep belief that literature is the best way to offer wisdom and sanity, countering a world where discontinuities and evil increasingly abound. A current concern is with the state of contemporary writing and some recent international fiction prize winners. He cannot fathom how some winners, often with indecipherable plots and pretentious prose, have won accolades by renowned judges.

Retirement gives Walter opportunities to set new agendas for living and relating. In the comforting surrounds of his study, he has laid down approaches to the future. Apart from catering for his physical well-being and being devoted to family activities, he sees importance in sustaining acuity of mind and taking up causes which promote civility and compassion in society. His first forays were involvements with the University of the Third Age, volunteering to teach English to immigrants and refugees as well as working with the local Community Law Centre writing submissions and reports.

Blessed with quiet and unobtrusive neighbours Walter enjoys the fruits of inner urban life, including proximity to the galleries, theatres and exhibitions. He keeps tabs on arts and literature through subscriptions to review periodicals and borrowing a friend's copies of The New Yorker. The decline in the standard of arts reporting in the local media annoys him, especially the pedestrian prattle and the self-aggrandisement expressed among arts reporters. Both he and his wife frequent the local cinema, enjoying the film festivals of European origin.

Unsettling Walter is the crushing wave of political correctness, the cancel culture movement and the insularity swamping public and private discourses. Freedom of expression and honesty are clear victims in his mind. He is startled by the number of times he notes friends correcting or censoring their conversations, striving to neutralise or remove strong beliefs and opinions from their utterances. Blandness and emptiness result. He watches in dismay as universities eschew formal pledges to guarantee freedoms of speech and association on their campuses. Deeply missed are forthright, reasoned and argued positions in public discourses.

At times when walking, Walter reflects on the kinds of thoughts pilgrims had, when they walked the pathways to their shrines. He tries to think about what is the spiritual feeling and well-being derived from walking. Apart from the euphoria from physical exertion, he senses that it pushes thoughts and musings into areas uncluttered by the press of urgencies and trivia of everyday life. It is easy to let the mind to float across the unusual and inconsequential. His mind has rambled through a diverse terrain of thoughts, including immortality, gender fluidity, life forms in outer space and witchcraft. An ambition is to walk one of the Caminos in Northern Spain.

Retirement and walking allow Walter to reflect on life. They help to gain release and respite, but former concerns still intrude.

Carol

Divorcee Carol is normally buoyant when she does her late morning routine of fetching two takeaway coffees from her nearby local cafe. The doubled-shot cappuccinos wend their way to her rented apartment, which she shares with fellow casino worker, Robin. Both divorcees had unhappy marriages and were permanently bruised by the experience. They became great pals when working the late shifts at the casino. Remarriage is considered but only on terms where respect and independence are secure. They both enjoy a good time. Carol misses male companionship but her dating has not led to an interest where she is prepared to invest her emotions and time.

Soon turning 48, Carol spends time and money to keep up appearances. She offsets her plump figure with slimline clothing and her puddingish face with styled, streaked hairdos and cleopatra-like eye shading. She adores funky jewellery, which consumes her special tips from the casino tables which she serves. The casino's manicurist and pedicurist enjoy her patronage. Conscious of weight, Carol goes on crash diets to prevent her breaking her desired weight limit of 69 kilos. Her physical activity is limited to coffee fetching and, where possible, clubbing and dancing.

Carol values routine and certainty. She dislikes the turnover of staff encountered at both the casino and her café. Acquaintanceship and familiarity are important. She is anxious when developing rapport with new fellow workers and café waitresses. Robin is an easy - going flatmate, anticipating and yielding to Carol's habits and routines. Although having a strong personality, Carol is seen by others as anxious and intolerant when faced with change. Others also see Carol as comfortable with a world which is black and white.

Raised in Dubbo, Carol had an uneventful upbringing, leaving home to work as a receptionist at a major city hotel. Her former husband, a casino worker, introduced her to work in the casino, where she progressed through a number of positions before working the tables. She returns to Dubbo to visit her widowed mother when there are family functions. Her mother, saddened by Carol's divorce, reminds, in an unsubtle way, that there are plenty of men in rural areas seeking a catch like Carol. But Carol sees little appeal in rural life, where the open vistas paradoxically offer a confining life.

In her job she has control, setting the tempo and building a courteous relationship with patrons. Management applaud her ability to connect with Asian patrons. She has a tense relationship with one of the female supervisors, and Carol, has at times, been tempted to tell her, sotto voce, to go f*** herself. Troubling Carol are her eyes which she knows require glasses, but vanity has put off getting attention. Some patrons have asked her out for dinner, but she politely declines under the excuse that this contravenes management policy. Her protection is to keep cross-table interaction limited to the patois of gamblers. She is no longer surprised by the obsessive behaviour of cultured and well-mannered patrons who are besotted with gambling.

Carol cherishes her friendship with Robin. They often go shopping, dining and socialising together. Robin normally accompanies her to factory shops, where Carol seeks slim-allusion clothing. They join girlfriends to have occasional dinners, favouring a number of middle-eastern restaurants where, apart from the exotic food, they relish the attention of waiters who charm and flatter endlessly. Carol was tempted to go on a date with one of the waiters but resisted, according to Robin, because of the alleged notoriety of middle eastern men's treatment of females. Her companions found her apprehension laughable and encouraged her to be more adventurous.

Proudly Australian, Carol loves to vent her views about migration levels, which she feels are too high. The crowded inner - city concentration of Asian migrants are often her focus. Many established migrants do not seem to have English proficiency, even though they have citizenship and settle in areas which are becoming mono rather than multicultural. She is not convinced that this concentration is temporary and she doubts that, in the long-term, whether some ethnic groups will disperse. Carol's concerns are equally shared by her mother.

A busy and exacting job, late hours and chores leave little space for Carol to weigh up the commitment options for personal development and well-being. She is aware that her friends, very transactional and day to day in their life choices, seem happy so long as their income and relationships are sustained. She often experiences uneasiness when she feels that her boundaries, personal and social, are too constrained and she experiences a sense of unfulfillment. From time to time she reads articles in the papers about how other people set up their agendas for life with apparent ease. She finds it hard to define what is missing but she knows that for her the answer is not in religion. There is frustration at not being able to put her finger on why she feels she is drifting and has no clear purpose in life.

Carol's mother nags her about being too obligated to her job and her friends, one of whom has allowed Carol to rent her flat for the past six years without a rent rise. Carol, feeling indebted, has spent lots of her own funds in decorating and furnishing the flat, as well as paying for all maintenance. Her boss has called Carol to cover for absent employees, even when she has exceeded both her normal and overtime hours. Even when she needs a break it is difficult not to accept the call and give up outings with friends. To say no is too hard. Her mother worries that she is too generous and is not allocating enough of herself to herself.

Carol is in a groove which is mostly agreeable. There is a desire to get out of her rut, but the road map for a more divergent life has not arrived.

Lina

Management graduate Lina works in her uncle's newsagency, while she continues to search for full-time professional employment. Entering her second year since graduation without a professional job has depressed Lina. She has started a part - time post graduate diploma to advance residency claims. Her Management Professor at her Broadway campus gave career guidance, but his suggestions were laughable, given the options for a young Chinese female graduate with no experience. In a way, she was not surprised since the Professor had never worked in business or management. Her uncle cannot help. He has no business networks and struggles with the English language. Her parents back in China are also worried that her degree studies have not yielded worthy employment.

At times Lina finds the counter work a chore, because she is reminded that professional full-time work has eluded her. Customers see a different Lina. They see a slightly built, dark haired, confident and poised young woman, forever courteous with sparkling eyes and a smiling, welcoming face which some customers liken to those beautiful Chinese courtesan faces seen in old Chinese paintings. Most times Lina does not wear glasses. Customers are pleasantly surprised at her English fluency.

LINA

Older customers enjoy her chatty disposition and her acquaintance with local stories and problems. When not busy she will have long chats with elderly customers, who linger for a friendly exchange or gossip. A continuing surprise is that many seem lonely and have no family.

Cushioned by a close friendship circle and her city flatmates, Lina is managing to weather the disappointment about employment. They also give her moral support, when pressures to return home and marry arise. Lina knows she could not stand the confining and monitored environment she would face with her family and their community. Her gregarious and shiny personality gives her an advantage over some of her fellow international graduates, who face difficulties warming to the idiosyncrasies of Australian culture.

Interactions with customers revised Lina's views about racism. Initially she had a negative view about her acceptance in Australia, but the experience at the newsagency has provided new insights. Customers are courteous and most always greet her warmly. She is surprised about their openness, divulging many aspects of their private lives, including their medical issues, spouse problems and the disobedience of their children. She is amused when older customers call her, 'darling', 'love', 'dear' or 'sweetie'. And she is amazed how much they spend weekly on lotteries.

Some young male customers have asked her for a date. One lady customer invited her to come home for dinner to meet her bachelor son. Flattered, she declined, allowing conservative and cultural imperatives to hold sway. Her only embarrassment has come from a customer, one of her former part-time lecturers at Broadway, who repeatedly asked her to join him for dinner. She always declined. He was hopeless as a lecturer and would be even more hopeless as a dinner companion. Sometimes dating requests remind her of her intention to find a marriage partner locally and settle down in Australia. At university she dated fellow countrymen several times, but found them dull, predictable and unromantic.

Visits to her homeland only strengthen her resolve to permanently settle in Australia. Life in China has lost its appeal in the light of the greater amount of personal space and freedom experienced in Australia. Even though her parents are relatively affluent and are generous, she cannot ever envisage finding a satisfying and fulfilling life in China. Her flatmates, through dinners, travel and parties, have exposed Lina to an open and engaged social life, which also afford the opportunity to retreat into her own world and have her off-beat views respected by her peers.

Spurred on by girlfriends, Lina enjoys fashion shopping when stores have sales. On social occasions, she has moved from sober dress styles to more colourful and feminine styles which show her figure to great advantage. One girlfriend has encouraged her to wear higher heels which, at first, she thought slightly silly, but is now a devoted convert. When working, she dresses conservatively to ensure there is no reaction from her uncle and his family.

Ever watchful, Lina is careful when socialising to assess political orientation when introduced to new people. She has encountered some Chinese seeking a permanent visa, who seem to be in a transitory existence, accepting the lifestyle and bounties of Australia, yet still holding strong yearnings and links to their homeland and its customs. Lina has many discussions with flatmates about them, arguing that they need to embrace their adopted country and jettison selective positive thoughts of life in their homeland. Lina has worried about China's actions in Hong Kong as well as the treatment of Uighurs.

Leisure time is important to Lina. Her favourite pastime is to experiment with cooking, including other Asian as well as Middle Eastern dishes. Her flatmates encourage her. One flatmate has introduced her to a friend, a young lawyer who has Iranian parents. He comes to dinner parties and urges Lina to try Iranian cuisine. He is unattached and she finds him attractive and interesting. Thoughts of a romantic link have loomed. She is summoning the courage to ask him to accompany her to sample some of the diverse cuisines of nearby low - cost eateries.

Lina discusses with her closest girlfriend the sort of work destinies she can reasonably expect, given her situation. Options and approaches to secure professional full-time employment are considered. Employment barriers are difficult to accept, given they are fluent in two languages and have good degrees. They are somewhat miffed that some of their classmates used family networks to secure satisfying work in Australian companies. Trying their luck in Britain, where other classmates have found work, has been considered. Holding them back is the lifestyle enjoyed in a comfortable and cosmopolitan Australia.

Lina loves life in Australia, but remains frustrated by the lack of professional work opportunities. Romance and perhaps overseas travel are possible lights on the horizon.

Cath

Kindly, energetic Cath looks forward to running the periodic Saturday charity stall, sited outside a local supermarket. Spring and autumn are her favourite seasons for stall work. She loathes summers and the inevitable humidity. Involvement in running a stall for 11 years gives Cath an opportunity to gauge the generosity of the public. In recent times she notes that mostly older people tend to patronise her stall, sharing a friendly chat and sometimes an enquiry about her health. Cath notes that many young adults are not inclined to support her stall and the charity. Child welfare and medical charities have been the areas most supported by Cath.

A long time Balmain resident, Cath also makes jams and cakes for stall sales. Her friend Barbara marvels at her industry and dedication, given that Cath is approaching her 70th birthday. Her thin, diminutive figure belies a strong, hardy and active person who gives her all to family, friends and causes. A marriage of 48 years, home duties, two children, and selfless support for her husband put Cath as the classic traditional homemaker. Now blessed with five grandchildren, the ever-optimistic Cath feels that she has been delivered a good deal from life. Husband Eric, a machinist for all his adult life, is also justly proud of the achievements he and Cath have made in owning their home and building a loving family.

The stall trestle table and the layout of its items are important to Cath, who insists there is order in the display. She is quick to identify unpopular items and always lets other stall volunteers and contributors know what sells best. Irritating a normally unflappable Cath are various advocate groups who crowd the precinct of the stall promoting their cause or seeking donations. Political and civic action groups annoy her the most. Friend Barbara often directs them to move to a more distant location. Sometimes Cath's teenage granddaughter will assist on the stall, and husband Eric erects and dismantles the stall.

The passing parade on a Saturday entertains Cath when, at quieter moments, she has time to observe the local citizenry. Young families with babies always bring a smile as do old friends and neighbours who pass by. The normally tolerant Cath is irked by the occasional, tatty pageantry of men and women whose hair styles, body jewellery, tattoos, or attire assail her sense of taste and decorum. She is repulsed by face-piercing jewellery, tattoos on the limbs of women, weird hair colouring and grotesque face make-up. Her granddaughter chides Cath about this, urging her grandmother to wear more colour and get her hairdresser to do something modern with her long grey hair which will highlight her doe-like eyes. Through encouragement by her granddaughter Cath has become an adept mobile phone convert.

Of late Cath has been reminiscing about early times. Her fondest memories as a young girl were the annual holidays at an aunt's house at Tuggerah Lakes with her parents and five siblings. There they played card games at night, while the day was full of swimming, canoeing and fishing. When the moon was right, all the family went prawning and most times there was a sufficient catch for a feast for lunch the next day. To this day she remembers the salty, fishy seaweed smell of the lake and the irritation of sand caught in her shirred swimmers.

Before marrying, Cath worked at a large department store in Sydney, first in haberdashery and then footwear. Regarded as a good sales lady, she was always receiving praise from her supervisors. Sometimes she would bring home a small treat from its food hall, including wedges of chocolate layered cake which her father relished. A recent visit to the store saddened Cath. Its displays, staff service and range of merchandise were not up to her standards. Sales staff seemed a disinterested lot. The feel and image of the store irritated. Adding to its demise were some internal layouts where exclusive sections, dedicated to branded apparel, gave the store the feeling of a tawdry bazaar.

A number of friends have been encouraging more adventures at her stage of life. Some have suggested going to Asia, others bus holidays around Australia, whilst others have sung the virtues of cruising the Pacific. All appeal, but a sense of obligation and apprehension constrain her. Husband Eric is not keen, because he does not want to leave his prized bird collection and aviaries for others to handle. As well, Cath feels that extended holidays are indulgences adversely affecting her family and charity work. Her sense of indispensability, which she openly rejects when challenged by her children, explains her reaction to holiday adventures.

Some major changes in routines have caused Cath to be unsettled about life. Husband Eric now sleeps in a separate bedroom, ostensibly because of his claim of restlessness and toilet calls, not because of romantic disinterest. Her children prefer texting to phone calls, her friends prefer morning coffee to tea, her favourite radio station now has switched to mindless talkback sessions, and banking and post office staff are annoyingly indifferent. More broadly she is disturbed by the decline of trust and honesty, especially when institutions and prominent people fail to uphold just and ethical standards. These changes are part of modern life, claims Barbara, but for Cath they are changes which she finds hard to accept.

Religion has not hitherto been important to Cath. Although baptised as an Anglican and raised in a religious family, Cath has felt no need for religious imperatives for her moral compass. Family and civic values have been important in guiding her views and behaviour. Recently though, and through contact with a charity friend, a Quaker, she has attended Quaker meetings when commitments allow. There she is surprised to find a spiritual uplifting, both clarifying her undisclosed life principles and her approaches to adversity and community failings. Family and friends are supportive of this new involvement, accepting it is consistent with Cath's character.

Buffeted by transitions in society Cath, sees a charitable outlook important to maintain a balance in her life. Supportive family and friends are important to Cath and serve to remind her of the joy gained from sharing and serving.

Sione

~ WASTE COLLECTOR ~

The nuggety 107 kg Sione is now in his second year of working on waste collection trucks operated by a local council contractor. He is thankful for the job, arranged through an uncle, because it allows time in the afternoon to spend with his music, rugby and family. Fellow workers like Sione. He is jovial and popular even though he doesn't share their enthusiasm for alcohol. Conscious of the need to maintain a relaxed relationship with colleagues, he occasionally joins them for afternoon drinks, when his 'tipple' is Coca Cola. At their local drinking hole, his group is known as the 'recyclophants', formerly referred to as 'garbologists'.

The 19 year old islander lives with his family in an old federation house at Lewisham, where they have lived on and off for nine years. Most times there is only his mother and two sisters at home, but numbers are bolstered when his father and brother return from off-shore rig work or when visiting relatives take up sporadic roosting. The house was owned by his late grandfather, who served as a minister of religion in a number of islander churches. Sione never shies away from his religious affiliation, withstanding the tormenting and teasing experienced both at school and work. His mother is not pleased that some of her Tongan family have become Mormons and now live in North America.

Sione's schooling was disrupted by illness and home movement occasioned by his father's work. His saving grace was sport and music accomplishments. Following on from sports at school and now at weekends, Sione receives praise for his rugby skills. Advantaged by some tutoring in guitar playing, he continues to practise and plays with a band at church and community social functions. Ever frustrated by his low academic achievements, he vows to go to college and get training in events management, which he knows from relatives is full of employment opportunities. For the moment, he cools his heels doing well-paid council work.

Orchestrating a social life is a challenge, following his girlfriend's move to the Central Coast, where she works as a veterinary nurse. Juggling time with her and between work, sport and church is becoming a challenge. He tries to fit some time on Friday and Saturday nights to be with her, whenever he can borrow his sister's car. He resists the pressure to share a flat with her and take up a more convenient job. For the moment, he enjoys independence as well as appreciating the household support by his mother, whom he worships. When his brother is working off-shore, he welcomes the privacy of their shared bedroom, where he can play and experiment with music.

His closest friend is a male cousin, who is an avid fan of traditional island music and dance. Sione is at ease with his cousin's homosexuality. They have gone clubbing together, especially enjoying band nights at nearby hotels. His cousin ribs Sione about his conservative clothing taste and closely cropped hair. Sione, conversant with Tongan cultural conditions and understanding, moves comfortably between the straight and gay worlds. They plan a trip to the USA, where Sione can attend grid iron matches and his cousin can explore his interests in the fusion between traditional and contemporary dance styles. Both are devoted fans of the 'Voice' and 'Survivor' TV programs.

Workmates are quite cynical about the recycling campaigns mounted by governments and environmental groups. Sione remains neutral on the issue. He understands their cynicism, having observed how communities do not heed collection protocol for bins, by disregarding waste sorting directions. Collection depots forward mixed waste to landfills. He is not overly surprised about how the recycling mantra is ignored, both by the waste producers and processors.

Whenever he thinks about work, he recalls the second day at work when he was subject to a prank. Half way through their collection run, his offsider yelled out that a body had been tipped from a bin into the truck. Sione looked and thought he saw a mangled figure. Alarmed he halted the truck and was told by the driver to ring the police. Just as he was about to report the body, his offsider removed it to reveal a disfigured female dummy model. It took a while before Sione appreciated the prank.

Despite beautiful stories about his mother's homeland, Sione has no great interest to visit. Mixed messages about conditions and lifestyle there do not inspire a visit any time soon. His elder sister has visited and became disheartened and somewhat disinterested in local happenings. There were few remaining distant relatives to visit. His father has never shown an interest for a visit. The cultural experiences, delivered through his local extended family and church association, satisfy for the moment. He marvels at the energy and devotion his local church leader continues to display on cultural matters. And he is surprised how much the congregation has grown over his time with the church.

Reflecting on his ambitions and prospects, Sione recognises that hurdles do exist. Blessed with a strong family, he knows he has been fortunate. Two of his second cousins, raised in dysfunctional families, are often on the wrong side of the law and seem aimless. He cringes whenever there are negative Islander stories in the media. His father, never without work and always responsible for family welfare, is an icon. Sione feels that he has his Dad's industry and his Mum's focus on the good and positives of life. They have become role models in their community. He resolutely defends his culture and has cautioned young cousins to be proud of their island heritage and always be especially respectful of those promoting cultural and church values.

Confident and focussed, Sione does not see any impediments to shaping his life and future. Bolstered and shepherded by a loving family, whilst experiencing affirming relationships at work and in the community, Sione has no reason to be apprehensive about new pursuits.

Wayne

Wayne has to pinch himself to remind of his good fortune. Happily married, two cooperative teenage sons, good health, a lovely home, a permanent job and financially security all make the 43 year old consider that he has been dealt a good hand. Now in his fifth year as a council gardener, he believes he has one of the best jobs any man would want. Working outside in council gardens and parks gives him a daily spiritual uplift which becomes more heightened in the transitions of seasons. He imagines foliage and flowers beckoning him into their midst.

The former bowling club greenkeeper receives regular compliments from his supervisors for his diligence and performance, which is reflected in the informal praise from the public for the garden displays and the landscaping around and in the parks. While Wayne works well with small groups, he prefers to work solo when an opportunity arises. He was offered but did not accept a supervisor's position.

At his bowling club he worked with part-time assistance. The club's closure following a sale to a real estate developer was a shock to him, given its apparent viability and stable membership.

Wayne is fit, athletic with a strong sturdy 90 kilo body, penetrating steel blue eyes, a craggy face and a determined jaw. He prides himself in maintaining a sensible diet regime and limits his alcohol to occasional beers with colleagues and when socialising at home. Warnings about skin cancers have been heeded and, for a long time, he has worn long sleeve shirts and wide brim hats. Younger work colleagues are urged to cover up to protect their skin. He prefers not to wear the fluoro vest issued by council.

In contrast to his bowling club, he has a continual challenge with minor vandalism, litter, and plant theft which usually occur at weekends. There is little problem with dogs, which are usually under control. The bane of his life are paper tissues and paper cups, which are dropped or are blown into the shrubbery. A further annoyance is to find human faeces behind shrubs. The park rangers keep the homeless on the move and they are rarely encountered by Wayne. His great secret is to allow locals, who have lost a loved one or pet, to privately spread the ashes in their favourite garden or shrubbery.

Staff slackness upsets Wayne. Many of his co-workers, even under supervision, lack commitment and are quick to retreat when the weather is unfavourable. Time allowed for mandatory tea and lunch breaks is abused and often they spend extensive time to prepare for knock off time. Initially Wayne commented to supervisors about this laxity, but found it achieved no result except for putting Wayne at odds with some colleagues.

Engaging with the public is always welcome by Wayne. In the parks and around the gardens, he encounters a cross section of the community, including seniors, disabled, young mothers, and the mentally disturbed. Some he sees regularly, particularly young mothers and seniors. When addressed, he engages in conversation which focuses mainly on plants and trees. One regular, who has a mental disability, comes and assists at weeding and sweeping under the guidance of Wayne. Some of the lonely park patrons are difficult to avoid. If allowed, they like to engage in lengthy conversations. It is at these times he wishes his plants could talk.

Troubling Wayne is the cost to council of materials, equipment and plants. He understands they come from two suppliers under competitive tender contracts. From his industry contacts, he knows that prices paid are well above industry benchmarks. He has raised this matter with management, who claim that this is outside their remit and in the hands of other executives. Wayne is wrestling with how to raise this directly with council. An approach to his local councillor was considered, but for now he has let the matter slide.

Weekend usage of parks has exploded in the period Wayne has worked with the council. Weddings, parties, family reunions and community displays are increasingly conducted, even though nominal charges are applied where use is of a commercial nature. Whilst most users leave parks tidy and clean, he notes that some ethnic groups are notorious for leaving litter as well as cigarette butts. Damage, though, to plants is minimal. He hears complaints from locals that the spring and summer weekends tend to have a lot of non-residents taking over the tables and shaded areas, even resorting to arriving early to erect shade awnings and to set down ground cover.

Wayne regrets that he never undertook formal college study of horticulture. Experience has provided good knowledge and skills, but he gets frustrated by not having more scientific appreciation of plant life and the array of chemicals used to manage garden and park botany. The council offered to pay fees for relevant courses to assist Wayne's work but, to date, home commitments have precluded consideration of this offer. Where possible, Wayne will use internet sources to deepen and extend his know-how.

The debate about climate change is a regular topic at home and work. He is not across all the factors giving rise to change and is unsettled by the different policy positions of political parties. His father points out the absurdity of condemning coal usage in Australia, while it is increasingly exported to Asia at record levels. He sees his responsibility, as a green conscious citizen, to participate in local initiatives to remove pollutants found in and around the parks. He is pleased that his council offers free garden mulch at its depots for all its householders.

Away from work Wayne loves his family life and their outside involvements. His sons play soccer, which he loves to watch as well as volunteering for their club to raise money through stall and raffle sales. Being the ultimate romantic, Wayne treats his wife with surprise gifts and vouchers to be redeemed at two leading ladies fashion outlets. They always manage each year to have a week away together interstate, leaving their sons with grandparents.

Outdoor work and immersion in horticultural tasks give Wayne never ending pleasure. The positive charge he gets from his work means he can enjoy home life and the social world beyond.

Sarah

A recently retrenched journalist and literature critic, Sarah, spends hours networking to seek a full- time professional writing job. Thankful that her parliamentary researcher partner, Tim, is able to support, Sarah nevertheless does not want to waste her skills developed over a 14 year media career. Whilst talking to friends and taking coffees with writer colleagues ease her unhappiness, she quietly seethes, wondering why she, and not less experienced and less accomplished colleagues, remains without a regular job. The reality of not working for the last two months has started to take hold, undermining confidence and denting her normal bubbling personality. She is often seen sitting brooding, while she observes the calming landscape at her nearby harbourside park.

At times she allows jealousy to cloud her normally positive and charitable character. Eating away at her feelings are the thoughts of how many less talented writers have found work with the public broadcaster or joined the flock of commentary media, where opinions are conflated with facts. Incensing her further is what now passes for good journalism. Shallow and incoherent writing now pass muster. What particularly grates her is how ethnic or gender categories appear to influence hiring decisions.

A bout of jealousy and too much wine recently put Sarah in an embarrassing situation where, at a favourite Thai restaurant, when dining with local media colleagues, she openly abused a fellow female journalist for spreading unhelpful views about her professionalism at a recent media conference. Tim, severely alarmed by this, had to coax Sarah to leave, whilst apologising for this unaccustomed outburst. It was totally out of character, and he was surprised when, subsequently, Sarah refused to recant or apologise for the outburst.

Pondering her age is not helpful to Sarah when considering the future. She wonders why a dynamic and successful career has put this 37 year old in this situation. Reports affirm her credentials, which are complemented by her stylish, youthful and feminine appearance. New acquaintances cannot believe she is in her thirties. Tim, in lighter moments, claims that Sarah's fiery red hair and piercing eyes make her a 'smashing sort' and a certainty for success in media work involving personal interaction. This does not give Sarah solace, as she mooches around after Tim has gone to work. Public relations, press agency, and corporate media work have been considered but, in Sarah's mind, they do not offer her scope for her talents.

A neighbour has asked her to do voluntary media work for a local action group, campaigning for more open space and recreation areas. At other times she would happily undertake such work but her mood cancels any urge to assist. Mindful of the changes in media employment opportunities, Sarah has considered a total switch in career, including teaching and on - line publishing. However, the realities and conditions of these are not enough to consider them further. She has even rejected some editing work from Tim's office.

Thoughts of writing a book to divert her attention from her situation have occasionally passed through her mind.

A notice from her school reunion group for a forthcoming weekend retreat in the Southern Highlands has given her a prospect to get away and suspend wallowing in self-pity. Contact with her school friends has been sporadic. She has dinner occasionally with her two closest schoolfriends, both of whom are married with children. These gatherings unsettle Sarah, reminding her of dreams as an adolescent of being a mother and wife. Career, events and relationships conspired to keep this aspiration just that. Her social circle never produced males with whom parenting would be attractive. Tim, a loving companion, would be a hopeless father.

Drinking nice wine for Sarah has always been one of the pleasures of life. Stress encourages imbibing. Tim has often arrived home to find Sarah in a near mindless state, with a near-finished bottle of her favourite brand of Pinot Gris and the TV burbling in the background. He feels like remonstrating, but understands that the employment situation has hit Sarah harder than he expected and he is somewhat puzzled by this retreat into wine and her emotional disarray. Sarah's maudlin state is concealed when she is out and about, and she reminds others that her talents will bring her work shortly. Sarah's mother senses her daughter's plight through the atypical tenor of her conversation during their weekly phone chat.

Undermining Sarah's outlook is the number of unanswered texts and calls made to contacts in the industry. Those who have answered remind her that senior positions are in short supply and that she will need to look overseas for opportunities which match her skills and experience. She has discussed with Tim about putting feelers out to international recruiters, but his body signals indicate that she would encounter problems with Tim if she seriously chased work abroad. In her present plight she is inclined not to ruffle Tim, who is offering lots of support. Her emotional dependence on Tim has surprised her.

Unexpectedly Sarah has found regular visits to a local beauty and massage therapy salon are the perfect antidote to periods of negativity. The pampering, body contouring and gentle pummelling surprisingly suspend her from her current woes. It not only distracts but generates a better feeling about herself, promoting thoughts that her setback is purely temporary. Her beautician's chatter also diverts. Topics encompass family, politics, and relationships. The problems the beautician is having with her boyfriend always entertain and compel Sarah to put her own life into perspective.

The way forward for Sarah remains clouded. Options are limited and past professional success no longer guarantees new work. Being tethered to Tim provides comfort.

Leila

Six years of counter work in post offices have not diminished Leila's enthusiasm for dealing with the public. Her parents, who migrated from India, encouraged Leila to take on this job, following an unhappy end to a marriage facilitated by her relatives. Childless, the 32 year old Leila was offered a postal job through a family connection. It proved to come at the right time, when the disappointment of her marriage had abated and she wanted to get out from under the feet of her parents, with whom she lived after her breakup. She found the interactions with counter staff and customers diverting, whilst providing the right tonic to ease her way back into life.

Leila did not inherit the beauty of her mother, apart from her mother's lustrous hair features. Her plain features were not helped by inheriting a strong resemblance to her father, including a heavy brow, oversized nose and elongated ears. Since her break up, she has gained weight with which her short stature has just managed to cope. Counter work has allowed her natural charm to flourish. Neither her parents nor her former partner encouraged her to explore life and she suffered from cultural and customary containment. Contact with the wider world has now unleashed a personality which had long been bottled up.

Leila

Initially, she followed the counter service protocol which the manager had framed for dealing with customers. The bureaucratic and indifferent behaviour this generated did not appeal to Leila. Gradually she developed her own style, which emphasised a welcoming smile and helpful propensity rarely displayed by fellow counter staff. Customers warm to her, preparing to chat about their views and experiences whenever the counter is not busy. She senses that some older customers are lonely and crave for a bit of conversation, and is incensed when a senior colleague will often close her counter to attend to back office matters even when the number queuing for service is growing.

There is an increasing frustration with the layout of the post office, which annoys her and many customers. Cluttered merchandise around the aisles and haphazard queue arrangements generate the atmosphere of a crowded oriental bazaar. Leila, as assistant, has to refrain from comment, as her manager takes great pride in his periodic rearrangements of aisles and queue lines. Frequently the merchandise stands are toppled by untethered youngsters as their parents wait for service. The presence of confectionery and toys in these stands also encourages toppling outbreaks.

Home life has been difficult, with her carrying the burden of a failed marriage which has led to parental coolness and suppressed criticism. Her married siblings, who visit regularly with their children, can unintentionally stir unease about Leila's situation. Leila will take herself off to the movies or visit an old schoolfriend on weekends, to escape the family tension about her marital disappointment. Her mother, understanding her situation, encourages Leila to join cultural groups to get a release from work and home pressures.

Leila has a strong desire to get married again and have children. Opportunities for meeting a future partner are limited, even though she is prepared to have a husband who is 'out of bounds', on traditional cultural criteria. Encounters at work and in the Indian community have yielded no prospects. She has toyed with the idea, if she had independent housing, to consider having a child through artificial insemination. She is desperate to hear the cry of 'Mummy' rather than the irritating tag of 'Aunty'. Online sites are being scanned to gather information on options to take this route to motherhood.

Conscious that her appearance is a factor in her work and community, Leila is spending more time and money on improvements. Her long hair is being styled to deemphasise her ears, her makeup offsets her facial prominences, jewellery is deployed to distract, and lipstick and nail colours added to suggest a more sensuous woman. Attacking her weight has been a challenge. One of her post office regulars, who runs a food preparation business is guiding Leila to desist from meals at home and switch to a helpful lunchtime diet. She swears that Leila's midriff will flatter again whenever she wears her traditional garb.

Leila feels that despite work, home and community life, she is living in a vacuum. The political, religious, civic and economic brouhaha which engulf the media and her family discussions do not rate in her mental landscape. It all seems repetitive and to no account. She likes to let her mind be consumed by the events and encounters of daily living. Sleep is rarely disturbed or troubled. Each day starts with a clean slate and her agendas, apart from the desire for romantic relationships, boil down to daily work, transport and family matters.

Unsettling Leila, though, are the images of young Asian women who feature prominently in leadership roles in commerce and government. They appear smart and mostly glamorous. While she knows that they have travelled pathways beyond her capabilities, she nevertheless wonders whether with a different upbringing, better schooling and without the hindrance of marriage, what kind of career may have been within her reach. While she loves her parents, she feels that their limited ambitions for her and their commitments to her brothers may have created barriers which she has unwittingly accepted.

Her work associates rarely talk about their private and family lives. Whenever Leila tries to engage in friendly conversations during her lunch break, she finds there is a reluctance to share their worlds. Leila, because work is one of her rare social exposures, is keen to understand how others conduct their lives away from work. Her married colleagues make no observations about their partners and will occasionally mention children whenever there is a celebratory event. This contrasts with the idle chatter of some of the older customers who, if there was time, would divulge happenings in their private lives without any prompting.

Leila understands that the post office is losing many of its key messaging and information roles. She wonders whether it could be a metaphor for life. She enters a changing world of contact, impersonal and technological, where real relationships are being eroded by communication gadgetry and isolation is on the rise.

George

~ HANDYMAN ~

Many households have benefited from the work and craftmanship of the multi - talented George, who has been a handyman in the district and nearby suburbs for seven years. Jobs come the way of George with little advertising. Sales staff of various paint, plumbing, tile, bathroom and kitchen outlets have no hesitation in providing George's business card when customers want small projects done. He outdoes his competitors in the word-of-mouth race. Apart from trade skills, his civility and personality make him a lay down misere for winning jobs even when price becomes a real consideration.

The former housepainter learnt trades informally, including a range of carpentry, plumbing, tiling and plastering skills when he worked as a trainee in his uncle's building firm. Following the collapse of the firm, he spent 15 years as a painting contractor, before the competition from Asian and Middle Eastern contractors made it difficult to compete. Now in his mid -forties, George is deploying all his experience and business knowhow to hold his share of the local handyman market.

George is proud of his Greek heritage but not overly so. He took some time to marry, despite three trips to his father's home island to find a bride. He travelled with the advantage of already owning his own four-bedroom home. Six years ago he was introduced to Despina, a niece of his uncle recently arrived from Greece, and within five months they were married. He is the proud father of two young sons. He considers himself fortunate. He was not blessed with good looks. His wiry body, dark complexion and off-putting facial features were always challenging. A misshaped ear, a squint and an over-squared chin did not help, he believed, in his romantic pursuits.

Through his upbringing, George always puts a lot of effort to make good and sustained impressions. He attends to presentation. Personal and business relations and dealings reflect his courteousness and trustworthiness. His business affairs are well organised. Family and friends joke about George's pristine work van where, with its special fittings and ordered layout, all his equipment and materials are clinically arranged and zealously maintained. They know that George's great reputation is widely known and are proud that he is known as a trusted and honest tradie.

Working hard has always been the mantra of George and his family. He was surprised, when visiting Greece, how many of the young men there seem to coast through life. Little industry and drive are witnessed among his age cohort there. Many could migrate, he knows, but too many seem to retreat and appear unmotivated to push through to a better life. However, he sees a lot to be proud about Greece, including commitments to family, community and culture. His two sons are learning Greek at home and at their special pre-school.

His cousins have asked George what has produced business success. To George it is a simple formula. You assure prompt household visits, timely precise quoting, phone follow-ups, completions on schedule, work guarantees, customer satisfaction checks and a New Year greetings card to new and former customers. Let your work sing your praise is George's advice. He also has what he calls a fine-tuned job pricing strategy, where all job aspects are detailed giving confidence that the job parameters are understood. He only commits to a job which can be managed within his time. Detailed invoices are always issued. He refuses to do 'cash jobs' to evade GST obligations.

Customers, in the most part, value his cooperative and consultative approaches. Some customers can be annoying and disruptive. In George's mind there are four types of these customers. There are the interferers, who interrupt work by requesting changes to work underway; the chatterboxes, who want to engage in conversation diverting attention from the job, as well as offering coffee and treats; the inspectors, who comment prematurely about job quality and progress; the agonisers, who worry about the impact or consequences of work in progress on family and household affairs. George's composure and professionalism manage to limit their impact.

The adjustment for Despina living and raising a family in Australia has been difficult at times. The language, absence of close friends, and some issues with the bossy nature of George's mother, have posed problems. George comforts her, indicating that in time she will find her feet and be able to handle his mother. George, though, has shortened his working day and is always home by 4pm to give his wife a break from the children. He plans to take her on a trip to Greece, once he feels his wife is settled to home making in urban Sydney. Wherever possible, they join Greek friends and relatives on weekends for lunches and social gatherings.

While George moves with ease amongst colleagues and customers, he continues to feel uneasy with aspects of some of the overbearing and insensitive behaviour of some Greek males, both friends and family. It seems sometimes that they have an arrogant bearing and seem not to comprehend the positive social changes in the roles and treatment of women. On occasions, he has upbraided uncles and others for the absence of respect and their lack of understanding of the dimensions of equality. This has got him into trouble whenever a wine-infused relative is offended by his views.

The conditions and scope of George's work afford him the flexibility to attend to personal and family matters. However, he considers what might be his work options if he finds he is no longer interested in handyman work. A couple of home building firms have offered supervisory jobs overseeing their projects. While flattered, he has seen these as unappealing, given his family situation. One option though is the possibility of joining his cousin, who runs an office redesign firm. There is the possibility of becoming a manager of operations, which he could conduct from home, scheduling building teams for each project. At the moment this remains in his mental in-tray.

George has ticked most the boxes for a good life, including steady and rewarding employment, a happy marriage with children, his own home and a nearby extended family. He knows that respect from customers will never be traded away.

Darren

Following a 15 year stint of long-distant truck driving, Darren is now in his fifth year of bus driving, mainly in Sydney's Inner West. The divorced 50 year old enjoys passenger interaction and is never flummoxed by traffic snarls and delays. Appealing is the mateship experienced at his depot, where there is constant humour and tomfoolery. He never complains about the schedules and routes on which he has been rostered. Truck driving, he believes, took years off his life, as well as bringing about his marriage failure. A blessing in a way was that his marriage was childless.

Darren lives with his older sister, after moving from Nowra following his divorce. He has Yuin heritage but has kept no links with his South Coast mob. He is unclear about some of his early ancestry, although a forbear may have been part Chinese, which is reflected in his facial features. For no reason Darren feels compelled to have fortnightly haircuts, when his moustache and eyebrows are also trimmed. His craggy face, steel grey eyes and strong, stocky body convey the image of a confident individual.

His sister works as a museum curator, specialising in indigenous artefacts. Slowly, she is coaxing Darren into thinking more about Aboriginal legacies and mythologies. While he has responded by accompanying her to various cultural displays, he feels troubled about their impact, given the lack of appeal to urban indigenous communities engrossed by the trappings of modern life. He and his sister, despite requests, have not joined a nearby activist group seeking redress on inadequate housing. His sister feels that advances in formal political status of their people are inevitable.

Darren remains troubled by his family history. He was raised by a devoted single mother, who never mentioned or connected with her family. Her only connection was with two so-called cousins, whom his mother visited. He asked about his father and grandparents but was told they were deceased. There were no photos. His mother alluded that she was fostered out but never retained a relationship with foster parents. Of late this has caused Darren sadness, when he and his sister reminisce about their late mother.

Driving buses and social interaction contrast with the loneliness experienced in long-distance truck driving. At the depot management directives, staffing rumours and union stirrings provide diversion, and depot relationships generate social opportunities and a welcome sense of belonging. Especially enjoyable and amusing is the human parade at the well-managed depot. He loves the multicultural, multi-gender, multi-age, multi-shaped, multi-political, multi-accent and multi-faith makeup of his co-workers. Each day always brings novelty either at the depot or on the bus.

Some mid-morning routes are special to Darren. Here he regularly encounters older and more colourful characters, contrasting with the early morning commuters silenced by their seemingly implanted aural technology or by their fingering of screens. Regulars greet him on alighting, and if there is no boarding queue, they will offer a comment on life, the weather or their current ailment. At Easter, he receives Easter eggs and, at Christmas, gifts of cake or small puddings from some of his older female regulars. Each Christmas he always installs a little toy plastic Christmas tree and Santa on top of the driver's entrance gate.

Darren has no tolerance for fare evaders. He is a legend at the depot for his action to remove evaders from his bus. He is known to not commence a journey, demanding that the transgressors leave the bus. Once he was cheered by a group of passengers when he directed two noisy adult evaders to alight, before journeying on. To date he has had total eviction success.

His sister is concerned about some of Darren's obsessions. He always carries a hand sanitizer. It is used before eating, driving and when leaving houses of friends. He is zealous with home duties, ensuring the kitchen, bathroom and bedroom are always neat and clean. There is no explanation for this behaviour because their mother's house was always untidy and housekeeping was haphazard.

Through his sister, he has occasional contacts with the Koori community. His sister is encouraging him to seek new friendships and a romantic interest in this community. Darren, somewhat shy and reserved in matters of romance, has not heeded her advice. The failure of his marriage and the relationship experiences of his mother have dampened any serious desire for long-term companionship, although of late he has had friendly conversation encounters with one of the depot female cleaners. This has rekindled some desire for female company and to consider the world of intimacy.

Darren does not share the interests of fellow drivers in scandals and politics. Even when truck driving, he could not get enthused about the endless complaints about police, supervisors and regulations. He didn't even share truckies' obsessions with country music and radio personalities. His one passion is for dogs, which his sister will not allow in her home. Before coming to Sydney, he always had a dog at home. They were always mongrels, providing him company and critical diversion from his failing marriage. Around his sister's neighbourhood he always will befriend dogs when he is out and about. Darren's new interest is basketball, which he catches on TV.

Troubling Darren is why he is indifferent to the emotional and political outpourings on indigenous rights, injustice, cultural appropriation and representation. He cannot assuage the historical discomfort of his mob. He understands their pleas, but does not want to invest time and energy in thinking about and committing to campaigns to bring change. His sister explains that his mother raised and educated them to be independent and self-reliant and, ultimately, it is your deeds and achievements which earn your place in society. Their mother held that relying on others is a copout and you must secure your own destiny. He senses that this could explain his persistent indifference.

Darren feels he is in control behind the wheel. Commuters and co - workers supply lots of joy. The support of his sibling is also cherished.

Jan & Kate

~ DISCORDANT NEIGHBOURS ~

A fence divides and contains. Jan loves her neat cottage with its groomed gardens, which she and her husband have painstakingly cultivated. Across the fence Kate and her various partners have neglected a garden that once enjoyed pristine conditions. From the road Jan's home radiates care and love, whilst Kate's dishevelled front yard suggests indifference and continuing neglect. Their open-railed fence fails to prevent the weeds, the wind-blown detritus and palm leaves of Kate's yard invading Jan's domain. This invasion has sustained a two - year continuous war of words. There is often silence between the ladies, who both celebrated their fiftieth birthdays within the last year.

Their fellow neighbours try not to take sides in the dispute, and are saddened that both ladies, who are fine people, cannot resolve their differences. Kate's domestic arrangements also irk Jan. Over the past six years since Kate took up residence, her home has seen the coming and goings of various male friends, who have obviously accepted the charms of Kate and her hospitality. Occasionally late evening loud music has Jan phoning the police to enforce silence. Jan's husband, Andy, does not engage in the disputes.

KATE

JAN

Jan's pride extends to her fashionable attire, which accentuates her compact, upright figure. Whether around the home or at work, Jan ensures her appearance will reflect her desire to always present the best possible image. Her short-cropped hair compliments her immaculate makeup to highlight her eyes and nose. Kate's tall and fulsome figure demand tailored garments which, apart from stressing her femininity, always give complement to her flawless complexion and striking shoulder length hair. Oft times, Kate eschews makeup to emphasise her starlet face. Neighbours conjecture that their differences in appearance suggest differences in some aspects of their character - Jan, aggressive and combative, if required, and Kate, easy going and bohemian, but in a positive sense.

Quarrels, according to neutral neighbours, are attributed to Jan's short wick. The venting of her displeasure at Kate's oversight or wrongs arise mostly on weekends when Jan does her gardening. If Kate is not outside Jan has no quandary about going next door and voicing her complaints. Kate mostly shrugs her shoulders and retires with minimum riposte. Jan has also detailed incidences in her emails, which generate no response.

Neighbours are amused at the tenor of Jan's language in her private accounts of disputes with Kate. Prefixed 'un' words regularly appear in these accounts, including - unashamed, unmindful, unceasing, uncharitable, unpardonable, unbefitting, untidy, unwarranted, unseemly, unthinkable, unsightly, unbearable, unending, and of course unneighbourly. Neighbours feel this is all too unfriendly and urge Jan to put matters in perspective and seek a more constructive approach to resolve the matters. They have given hints to Andy to dampen down Jan, but this has been to no avail.

Kate on the other hand, does not mull over such incidences. She is putting her companionship agendas to the fore, seeking a more adventurous life as reflected in her job as a travel consultant. Unknown to Jan, Kate spends little time reflecting on the disputes. Boyfriend issues and relationships occupy the mind of the three-times divorced Kate. The longest time she has sustained a male friend was nine months but this relationship was doomed early on, because her mate had no work and tested her finances too often. Kate is not a heavy drinker, but is a flirt, causing neighbourhood wives to remain on watch. She is an enthusiastic greeting embracer and energetic fareweller at social encounters, especially with male neighbours.

In contrast many see Jan as somewhat formal and aloof. Working as a senior paralegal in a large law firm has boosted Jan's sense of right and wrong, which her forlorn and corralled husband can readily attest to. Always ready to offer a legal opinion whenever asked, Jan draws admiration from neighbours when seeking advice on domestic and bureaucratic laws.

Jan enjoys local social gatherings, but positions herself to skirt the orbit of Kate if present. Even at the most informal gatherings, Jan's high-heeled, smart casual teeters on the brink of being formal. Her husband, whose pressed shirts and ironed slacks are inevitably accompanied by his imported Italian loafers, complements their appearance. Kate, on the other hand, pushes the fashion boundaries on colour and revelation. Her home crafted outfits help shelter her ampleness. She is a dynamic circulator and ensures she touches base with everyone before neighbours disperse.

Rosalie, a friend and nearby neighbour of both Kate and Jan, tries to limit friction, suggesting that Kate hires someone to periodically tidy up her gardens and yard. Kate has done so but frequently her busy engagements lead to periods of oversight, bringing back unkemptness and consequential dissension. Rosalie has pointed out to Jan that Kate is a good-hearted soul and has not a mean streak in her body. And after all, no one is endangered or hurt by the occasional vegetation invasion. But for whatever reason, Jan cannot let such matters rest.

While silent on Jan's quarrelsome forays, Andy would love a normal neighbourly setting, where he could treat Kate as a friend and where Jan would desist from her actions. Unknown to Jan, Andy has enjoyed several conversations with Kate, when sharing a bus commute to town. They chat about local matters but make no reference to Jan. They found they shared a love of modern jazz and an admiration for the same performers. Andy is not surprised that these encounters have brought the odd 'testosteronic' shudder. Whenever there is an opportune moment, Andy tries to remind Jan, without reference to neighbourly issues, that they are blessed to be living in a great locality, where a host of civic benefits are enjoyed.

There is all likelihood that Jan will not stop her protests and Kate will press on enjoying life while remaining undiverted by parochial bickering.

Leanne

Freckled-faced and somewhat sullen, Leanne has weathered bank organisational turmoil and the third rearrangement of the counter, office and entrance layouts of the branch, where she has worked on and off for 11 years. Personnel have also changed frequently, where managers, advisers and tellers seem to be pawns on a staffing chessboard. Lines of communication with various bank operations seem in constant flux and staff, like customers, are often at the mercy of a phone response. Older customers, having floundered with their cascading home internet prompts, are often seeking assurance that their security is not compromised by input errors.

Her branch is surrounded by many empty shops, reflecting changes in shopper behaviour and the impost of high rentals. The assortment of customers includes the solitary, the feckless, the forlorn, the eccentric, the profligate, the gasbags, the dilletantes, the snarlers, and the tightwads. Leanne always notes the dress of customers. Whilst casual dress prevails, there remain a few whose attire is classy and fashionable. She is surprised by sockless men in smart outfits and the increasing number of women who wear outsize jackets to hide their ampleness.

Unseating and unsettling Leanne's approach to her job has been the cultural mix of fellow workers. Acceptance of difference in the work place has been the not-so subtle messaging in staff training. But Leanne senses there is less emphasis on those shared values to make the work place collegial and reflective of the Australian way. Especially irksome is the disparaging manner of some Asian male staff, who leave her with a feeling of being denigrated and disrespected. Often it is not words but body-language which carries the venom of contempt and disapprobation. And this becomes exacerbated when carried out by a supervisor. Leanne has kept her powder dry when she encounters this behaviour and mulls over what to do, given the remote bureaucratic nature of regional management. She knows other female colleagues have had the same experience but rarely comment on the matter. Ironically the bank boasts about its extensive inclusive strategies, but fails to monitor the human resource and staff relations issues adversely affecting branch operations and relationships.

Bank changes could be considered a metaphor for Leanne's personal journey. Now just turned thirty, weight gain, early arthritic pain, troublesome eyesight, and unsettled hair style challenge her confidence. Movement in housing and relationships have not helped. Since leaving home at 20, she has moved flats five times through rental and flatmate problems. Her romantic pathway is strewn with relationship potholes. The last two boyfriends disappointed and, like the ones before, seemed incapable of committing to the cause of caring love. Her much older flatmate has criticised Leanne's club date-hunting modus operandi, suggesting she moves to dating sites to find Mr Right.

Leanne's mother claims that working in the bank has dulled her personality and promoted indifference.

Some friends have noted also that her effervescence and quirkiness have lost their edge. This was evident among her netball friends, who also have observed a change. Her netball period, which lasted four years after leaving school, was a high point in her life. Apart from the camaraderie, netball provided opportunities to express her competitive and organisational talents, which have been frustrated in her work situation. Over time Leanne has somehow allowed her work environment to stifle and contain her spirit and character.

Not conscious of these observations, Leanne endeavours to keep her appearance attuned to fashion changes and to follow bank guidance on how to give positive images to customers. Despite this, Leanne has developed an air of remoteness, which work colleagues interpret as being haughty and self-absorbed. Generally, there are no qualms about her work which is normally flawless.

Lunch break has given a lifeline in a friendship with Gail, a local worker in a lunch bar, who has encouraged Leanne to talk about her challenges and feelings. The friendship, which is now a year old, has given Leanne an opportunity to test reactions to her views about the bank and her experiences with flatmates and boyfriends. Gail, a social media addict, has plenty of advice and suggestions on how Leanne can move into new spheres, particularly groups offering cultural engagement through singing and theatre. Gail, a member of a pop choir, thinks Leanne's diffidence to new experiences can be breached if she joins her group.

Leanne has considered a change in career. Her approach to two job placement agents did not give a sense that there were attractive work options for her. The female agents were unenthusiastic and unimpressive. Both were clearly younger than her which she found off-putting. Their power outfits –

both had black trousers, black high heels and white blouses with turned-up collars-left Leanne cold. They laboured the obvious-Leanne's experience was narrow and her lack of tertiary studies was an impediment. One irritated especially. She kept glancing down to her mobile during the interview. Galling Leanne was that she had paid to get a professional to craft and write her resume and yet it appeared to not stir her agents. Not one job interview resulted.

The way ahead is somewhat murky and Leanne wonders whether her situation and a desire for a change are shared by other single working women in their thirties. New destinations - work, relationships, lifestyle, residence pop up regularly as future options for a change. If she is to make changes then she needs to do so while she has youth on her side. Holding her back is the security of income she enjoys with the bank. Friends tell her that while greener pastures might lie ahead, there always remains the real challenge of securing reliable income to support living. She is somewhat risk averse on financial matters, placing a real barrier on taking on the unknown.

Leanne feels that she is manacled to her job and is unable see a way through to achieve a new life. She shares such dilemma with others and wonders whether she is experiencing the late arrival of a quarter - life crisis.

Eddie

Locally born and raised Realtor, Eddie, knows his pitch like the back of his hand. Every street, lane, and park of his territory are indelibly imprinted in his head. All properties for sale or development, actual and potential, are etched in his brain and updated relentlessly as he navigates his urban borough in his leased 5-series BMW. He is a master of networking and the cast members in his property variety theatre - builders, architects, town planners, vendors, tradies and activists - all have a key role on his stage. Eddie believes he is the property impresario without peer.

There is nothing that seems to inhibit the foxy-faced Eddie. He has not been held back by an indifferent performance at school and college, a dysfunctional family and upbringing, two messy childless divorces, several failed business partnerships, a bantam roly-poly physique and several attempts to deregister his agency. He has factious relations with other local realtors. One former partner called him the Fred Astaire of property, through his seemingly endless steps to dance around ethical and professional standards. Some competitors view him as a cagey schemer. A key asset is his unencumbered main street office building, which he inherited from his father.

A survivor of two heart attacks, the 46 year old Eddie gets lots of encouragement from his younger, newly minted wife, Julie, who reveres his flair and expertise on all matters real estate. They met at a property launch, where Julie was drawn by his ease of mingling with the gathered invitees. Following a whirlwind courtship, the former podiatrist divorcee found herself at the feet of a bungalow purveyor, whose wiliness did not affect her admiration. She is not troubled that she overshadows Eddie by many centimetres and her lean physique is in contrast. One habit of Eddie endears. Without fail on Saturday nights, she receives fresh flowers accompanied by short love couplets penned by unknown versemongers. The fact that this is a standing order with a florist, who is a tenant of Eddie, does not diminish their appeal.

Currently the agency employs two sales executives and a property valet. The latter, developed from an idea of Eddie, has the task of shepherding prospective clients through property, both through on-site and on-line approaches. The ever-alert Eddie has not allowed the internet to outflank him. Whilst he embraces the new media, he remains the archetypal hands - on exponent. Publicity gambits involve free giveaways, including shopping bags outside supermarkets, non-disposable coffee cups, caps for local festivals and T - shirts for sports events. The costs have been funded through profits, made by his jointly owned import business, which sells promotional apparel made in Asia.

Eddie is not uncomplicated. He has been unaccountably abrasive with colleagues when plans go awry, and his employees have encountered his short fuse. Some business associates find him overly brash and aggressive, whenever he has to make a point. At social gatherings, the confidence exuding from Eddie has been known to be off-putting and is seen as arrogance. But charm always comes to the fore when deals and networks are underway. Julie accepts this harder side of Eddie, who remains high on her romance meter.

Eddie is aware that former colleagues believed he had a Napoleon complex. His nickname at school was 'Squirt' and he suffered derision about his short stature. His guile plus self-confidence enabled him to surmount school and early career setbacks. In business, he secured success through being the consummate dealer, where seller and buyer both emerge believing that they got the best outcome. Earlier in his career he wore built-up shoes, but gave them up when colleagues pointed out other notables, who are vertically challenged, succeed in government, business and politics. However, whenever he organises professional seminars, he always ensures they are seated affairs and he occupies height-boosting chairs.

Relations with local politics and politicians have been fitful. Alert to community suspicions about property developers' and real estate proprietors' dealings with government, Eddie has kept an arm's-length relationship with politics. Instead he cultivates, through donations and free management services, those lobby and activist groups able to put political pressure on matters where he has a potential interest. He was able to donate to a disability association a fully equipped learning centre which was part of his controversial, yet successful, light industrial development. It had opposition from the Mayor's political party, but was countered by the association's full and public support. Eddie has endeared himself to activists by publicly opposing all high-rise residential developments around parks and waterways. His vocal opposition to high rise has earned him the eponym, Scything Eddie.

A love of cricket has sustained him over the summer. At primary school, he excelled at cricket, especially with the bat, but lost interest when unhappy home and high school events unsettled his life. After high school, he played some social cricket, but the pressure to earn income and establish a home left little time for leisure. Once established in business, he has supported local teams through equipment purchases. All forms of cricket appeal and he never misses the first days of a test in Sydney. He attends charity lunches with cricket stars and has sold several properties to current and past cricket test players. Julie loves the cricket memorabilia Eddie has accumulated and loves the old sepia photos of the past greats of the game.

The nagging regret Eddie has is that he has never got in touch with his mother, who left the family following a bitter divorce, leaving ten year old Eddie in the care of his father. Eddie is unsure how to link up with her. She has never contacted him since leaving. He has driven to her address but was fearful to go and introduce himself. While Julie believes he should not agonise about this, he sometimes feels that his identity remains incomplete by not having connected. He feels there is an emptiness in his life and believes that the absence of a bond with his mother maybe its root cause. His dealings with families of clients serve to remind him of the importance of a loving mother.

Eddie has his professional domain well under his surveillance. In most respects his strategies provide a competitive advantage. He has overcome adversities, but has a lingering issue in achieving closure with his mother.

After Thought

ON URBAN SPECTATING

Urban settings facilitate spectating through the conditions of concentration, recurrence, regularity, congregation, channelling, congress, interdependence, patterning, and transacting. There is ample opportunity to closely encounter fellow citizens going about their everyday life.

Noting and observing urban strangers stirs curiosity, generating an urge to selectively meditate about their character and their daily happenings. A diverse universe of citizens transacting life is imagined.

Through imagination a mosaic of citizenry produces a human map, often revealing shared clusters of behaviours and viewpoints, influenced by urban experiences. The observed unwittingly yield insights into lives through disclosed features, including gestures, gender, gait, grooming, garb, girth, grace, guise and incidental gabble.

The observer can also personally benefit, through reflecting on life through the agency of spectating. Watching fellow citizens prompts thoughts about one's own led, and to be led. By speculating about their lives, a contra flow of ideas is generated about the observer's own life. This may prompt the observer to take stock of life.

About the Author

The writer came to Balmain district in 1990 where he has lived since. He was a financial educator, writer and consultant. His writing has appeared in journals, texts, and monographs. He has lived and worked in the Pacific, New Zealand, Britain and USA.

Outside family, travel, writing, and golf, Roger's current interests include researching the histories of Colonial NSW and Huguenots.

Roger Hugh Juchau (1941-) lives in Birchgrove and Wallaga Lake Heights, NSW.